Misguided Trust

LAUREN WAGNER

Chapter 1

United Region Water Laws: Established May 2167

Water restoration and conservation laws formed with the intent to restore and maintain the physical and biological integrity of the nation's waters are our nation's highest priority. Any ill citizens will be removed from government-proclaimed safety zones for the public's well-being.

Black SUVs line the street, their dark tinted windows and their sparkling silver rims reflecting impending doom. But the windows cannot keep out the screams. Not the cries, nor the banging from inside the vehicles. It's random health inspection day, and dozens of citizens have already failed, by the count of SUVs.

Josh stands to greet me with a kiss on the cheek, his silence speaking louder than words. I smile back and try to ignore the ominous SUV's and to ignore what is happening.

"Sit down. Don't draw any more attention to yourself than necessary," Josh says.

My pulse is pounding, and my chest rises and falls quicker than I can control. Sweat drips from my brow. My stomach is tied in knots. I assess my body for early signs of illness. No sore throat. No muscle aches. No nausea. All I can do is wait in silence. Our words would be lost anyway, so I sit down at the table.

I scan my surroundings and focus on the young girl walking down her front steps. She does not struggle. She does not cry or scream. She doesn't even whimper. No more than twelve, and she has already accepted her fate. She walks with her chin down, her eyes on the steps ahead. She opens the door to the parked car herself and climbs in.

There will be no conversations over breakfast this morning. There will be no laughter or small talk. Ordering food will be a futile task. No sane person could eat with their neighbors being hauled away.

Fear of the health inspections would be bad enough if only today were not the day I promised Maddox a fresh drop. Three weeks have passed since my last drop, and the last I spoke to him, I promised I only needed two. But I could not pull it off in time. Lucky for me, he isn't one to hold grudges. Any help he can get, he takes. Today will either be my luckiest day or my last day.

I drop my bag under my chair as nonchalantly as possible. I feel the weight of it as I kick it under my chair.

"Stop freaking out. You're fine," Josh says.

"What about you? Are you fine?"

"I'm not sick, Sara. And neither are you. Take a deep breath and pull yourself together."

A shrilled scream echoes down the street. My head snaps up to see a small, middle-aged woman hauled from an apartment complex. She struggles as two men, black jumpsuits covering them head to toe, push her along and throw her into the back of the closest SUV. Her muffled screams continue as she bangs on the windows. They walk away and move into the next building. I wonder if the young girl's disposition changes after being in the same car as this frantic woman.

Josh and I sit in silence, staring at the black SUVs. We both know the health inspectors will reach our small table in a few minutes. All the other tables outside the café's veranda remain empty. Even the inside tables lack visitors to help distract my frantic thoughts.

The green armbands around their biceps haunt my dreams, like a tightrope squeezing from polar ends or a noose twisting at my neck. Both of my parents were euthanized due to failed health inspections. I was orphaned because of days like today.

My fists clasp together as two health inspectors cross the street and approach our small table. I let my nails dig into my skin, a small but painful reminder that I need to keep it together, just as Josh said. My toes curl inside my shoes, and I clench my thighs to keep from shaking.

"Health inspections. Your full cooperation is expected."

On instinct, we stand as both men grab hold of our thumbs. Our prints are scanned on a hand-held device, and our mouths are swabbed. The health inspector's hand forces my mouth open, and I am left to stare at the SUVs down the street. Wondering. Were my parents the frantic type? Or were they calm and steady? I imagine my dad was the calm one and my mother frantic. But then again, I have no way of knowing. Memories erase themselves over time. I remember more about my mother's best friend Meredith picking me up from school that day than the scent of my own mother. It's a pity, really. The memory of Meredith is just as heartbreaking.

The inspector drops his hand from my mouth and pushes me away. I stumble in surprise, topple over my chair, and trip over my hidden belongings. My bag rolls underneath the table in response. Food rations and vitamin waters spill out of my small backpack, instantly exposing my treason.

Josh notices the spill. With eyes bulging, he glares at me. If I am caught with the extra food rations, I will be finished for sure.

"What the hell!"

Josh falls to his knees to meet me eye to eye. He pushes the table to its side, momentarily blocking the inspector's view of my recklessness. He yells at the inspectors with his knees landing directly on top of my spilled bag. "Since when is human indecency a part of your job?"

"Sir, we were not finished. We expect your cooperation."

"The hell, you will!"

"Is there a problem here?"

I turn my head to see a new enforcement officer approach. Not more than a year or two older than me and far too young to be out of school, the red arm-badge is the only indication of his position.

Enforcement always leads to trouble—no matter what color their arm badge. Say the wrong thing, and you'll be arrested in a second. Look at them the wrong way, and your swab might become accidentally infected.

The new officer places his badge on the table next to us and moves toward our flipped table. I make a point of not looking at the badge and give him a good look up and down instead. Blue-collared shirt, blue jeans, and an unshaven face. I expected an enforcement cop to at least brush his hair and tuck in his shirt.

Handsome as he may be, no one's luck ever turns out well with enforcement. And my day is not looking very lucky.

"No problem here, sir. Random health inspections. We just had a short trip of the feet, is all."

Both health inspectors stand rigid with their arms at their sides, waiting for a cop twenty years younger than them to decide their fate.

He looks past Josh and stares directly at me. "Is that true?"

My eyes read into his, and I wonder. Am I being baited? Sweat beads down my forehead as I consider the bag's weight underneath the table. He must have seen the goods. Josh must know it, too. I feel it in him next to me.

"Yes, sir," I say.

"And?" he says to the health inspectors.

"She's clear, sir. We haven't finished with him yet."

"Well then, let's keep moving," he says.

The two inspectors move in, but the enforcement officer remains with his eyes locked on mine. After what seems like several minutes, his eyes move to Josh. Josh waits silently like a perfect soldier.

They swab his cheek once more and glare at the readings on their hand-held device. The bastards are hoping he is flagged.

"All clear."

Without uttering another word, all three officers turn and walk away.

Josh and I sit down, waiting in stillness until the street clears. Seven SUVs drive away. I'm not sure how many people they hold. It's almost better if I don't know.

Josh's voice is barely audible as his temper flares. "What the hell are you doing with those rations!"

"What the hell were you thinking talking to enforcement like that?" I say in response.

"You're going to get yourself killed. Whatever you're up to, get over it and take those things home."

I ignore his comments and sit without a response. I knew he would be angry if he ever found out. But some things, a lot of things, are bigger than him.

"Fine. Give me the bag. I'll take them home for you," he says.

"No. Someone… is expecting them. It may not be much, but I do what I can. I have to." We whisper even though the street has cleared. Both of our tempers rise.

He takes a deep breath and shakes his head at me. "I'm not hungry." He stands up from the empty table, slams his chair in, and leaves.

As he walks away, all I can do is sit there. I would much rather he soothed my fears today than have a temper tantrum. Such an easy temper to get a rise out of, but I still hate being the one who angers him.

Breakfast is an obvious failure. I stand up and walk in the opposite direction. I pass the center of town, where the cop statue stands in front of the enforcement offices that stubbornly refuse to decay with the rest of the damn town. I'd spit on it if I thought nobody was looking, but somebody is always looking. I pass the injury ward and follow the silent street past the row houses that represent so much of Zone Three. A quiet town, where people are afraid to talk, laugh, or cry, even in the middle of the morning, when the streets remain deserted. People are already locked inside for the day, away from wandering eyes.

I slow to a deliberate stride at the northwest corner of town and scan the street behind me before tossing my bag of rations over the ten-foot metal railing. I walk away.

"The day you were born, the sky sang out with joy. The clouds danced

across the breeze straight to the ocean and announced your arrival." My mom brushes my hair as she gets me ready for bed, her voice as soft as the feathers in my pillow.

"Why the ocean, Ma? We don't live anywhere near the ocean."

"The ocean started as the purest place here on Earth. It's where the animals were born, where the mountains formed, and where all souls float ready to start their new lives."

"Is it still that way?"

"No, my dear. Once the water wars ended, the oceans were cut off from the rest of the world. At first, the wind cried. But after some time, we learned new ways."

"Do you think the ocean is mad at us?" I say.

"No, my dear. The ocean is waiting patiently for us to rebuild the world and absolve our mistakes."

"I wish I could go to the ocean one day," I say.

"Me too, darling. Me too."

Chapter 2

Interfering with water restoration and conservation laws is strictly prohibited.

I scrutinize the large mahogany desk positioned before me as I sit in my shrink's office later that afternoon. The legs curve out into claws with such immaculate details. I can't help but wonder if the claws are supposed to symbolize each one of her patient's secret desires to claw away at their skin. It's morbid, really. It just makes people yearn for it more, long for the inevitable pain that accompanies the fight. Place a sword in a knight's hand, and he will want to fight. Put a claw in a psychiatrist's office and make it resemble a razor blade.

"Sara? Sara, are you even listening to me?"

Dr. Hammid slides her glasses down her nose and glares at me. The black rims make her face look pointy and sharp around the edges.

I look up at her without changing the expression on my face. She is an older woman with wrinkles forming around the smile lines on her face. Her short hair makes her look captivating. She is actually brilliant, in small doses. And only brilliant on the days I am willing to listen to her. It's like eating a piece of chocolate. Tasting one makes you want another, but it leaves you feeling nauseous after a handful.

"I think we need to take another look at our treatment plan."

The look of concern in her eyes spreads across the room as if it were a tidal wave meant to decapitate me.

"No." I roll my eyes and slide into a deeper slouch. "Sorry, Doc, but no. I'm not changing anything anymore. Maybe this is just me. Maybe this is just the personality I am stuck with for the rest of my life, and maybe this is the best it gets."

Maybe I should stop coming to see Dr. Hammid. It's obviously not working. I wonder how long it will take for the government to chase after me if I stop mandated treatment.

"It always gets worse before it gets better, Sara. You have moved past the tears, the anger, and the immobilizing emotions. The acceptance is there; I just want you to be able to verbalize it."

She's right, of course. I have accepted it. I've just accepted something very different than what she is talking about. I've accepted that I feel better sad. That sadness is a part of me, and without it, I feel lost. I feel like I have abandoned the only part of me that I can truly count on, and without it, all I have is emptiness.

"Isolating yourself from the world doesn't change your past. It just prevents you from making a future," Dr. Hammid says.

I nod as if this is a profound thought I internalize.

I leave her office, contemplating how long this will last. I'm forced to visit her every other week, but I'm also forced to send blood samples every other day. One small prick on the finger, and I drop the vial into my mailbox. One more way for the government to control things that are none of their business. It is how they rationalize my living within the United Region Clean Zones. It's also how they justify my citizenship. I should have been locked out two years ago. I should have been left to die, just like Tommy.

Now, the only way to prove my mental stability is to prove I'm medicated. Honestly, it's not even the medication I mind. I can at least function now, whereas two years ago I was like an empty shell waiting to crack. But it bothers me that I was never given a choice.

While I head for a bench in the nearby park, the food trucks make their weekly deliveries—more rations to replace the ones I tossed over the fence. More rations I can't force myself to swallow. I'd rather starve in here to prove a point than feel grateful for the load of bullshit they deliver to every door. Food included.

Our ancestors survived just fine for thousands and thousands of years. People always came out on top despite bouts of war or minor incidents of environmental disasters. Until, of course, the nuclear war destroyed most of the world. Too many countries had access to weaponry which never should have existed. We doomed ourselves from the beginning.

After the war, the Earth's freshwater supply dropped to dangerous levels and forced our entire government structure to change. The government now controls every ounce of food and water that enters a person's home. Once we reach our daily water quota, they turn off our pipes, just like that. No warning, no explanations. It's all about numbers and conserving the planet.

Food rations are strictly monitored. Supposedly, if I eat everything they give me at the exact same time every day, my health will be perfect, forever. But it's crap—all of it. Food included. People outside the safety of the Clean Zones don't care about food taste. To them, it's a meal they don't need to worry about.

Five different Clean Zones house the citizens of the United Regions. And here in North America, they are the only places where water is safe. If you are not inside, you are as good as dead. Zone Three, where I live, was known as Chicago before the world was destroyed. Now, it is just a number. Three. A number that houses a few thousand people.

The truth is, Josh and I are the lucky ones. We can afford to eat out at public kitchens and cafés. We can look at a menu and select what we eat. It is a luxury, really. At least until my funds run dry. Most of the citizens in Zone Three are not entitled to the same indulgence. Our town may be wealthier than others, but we still have our pockets of poverty. They eat what the government tells them to eat day after day.

The United Regions is based on a two-tier system. At the head, Water Systems Inc. ensures clean and safe water purification. They have a massive piping system channeling water from the lakes, cleaning it, and pumping it out to those in the United Region. The second tier is the systems government, which enforces laws and initiates punishments to preserve the planet's water at all costs, like health inspections. To stop death in the world, we now create it. We only feed and nourish those the government deems as deserving and worthy of life.

Josh works at the mainframe out of Zone One. He does not talk much about his job. I know he does not believe in the whole system, but he would never verbalize his feelings.

But a job is a job. And in our new world order, people need a good job to keep up with water payments. But he worries about the people struggling outside the Clean Zones. I just know it. After what happened to Tommy… how could he not?

I go about my day as though living in a community behind locked gates doesn't matter. As if the constant fear of death doesn't put weight on my shoulders. But I hate living here. I hate the idea of Clean Zones. Rather than searching out the sick or deprived inside the zone, the government should be outside trying to find more safe water sources.

Once, I was not locked on the inside. I was one of the few who lived outside the safety of the Clean Zones. Or tried to live, anyway. The Outside may not have been safe, but I lived a freedom many people do not get the chance to experience. I made my own choices every day. And I miss it. I miss every second of it.

The imaginary smell of ash in the middle of the night from dimmed campfires often keeps me up at night. I slip out of bed in search of the smells, knowing I will never find the source because campfires are not allowed inside the gates. I was dragged from the Outside into a Clean Zone, despite me kicking and screaming. My freedoms were lost, and I was forced to stay. I was told my opinion did not matter. Frank, the man who raised me, had complete control over where I lived.

People whisper and move away from the old park bench I find myself on. They are the people who knew Tommy and me as one, and they probably blame me for his death. They won't voice it to me, though. They won't even talk to me. When I came back from the Outside, they picketed outside my window. They thought I shouldn't have been let back inside the gates. Truth be told, I wish I weren't.

"Can I sit?"

The weight of the hundred-year-old bench shifts under me. I drop my knees from my chest and attempt a stance that represents more confidence than I currently feel.

"No. I would rather you not," I say.

"Lucky for me, I don't need your permission."

The same enforcement officer from the café speaks to me differently than anyone who knows me, and it hits me. To the man sitting in front of me, I am not broken or fragile. I am no longer pitied or neglected. I am the girl who does not want to be here, and I am the girl who is constantly breaking the law.

Now dressed in a uniformed black jumpsuit, red bands adhere to his biceps. A bronze badge is secured to his chest, and he wears the same young, unshaven face.

"Can I help you somehow?" I say.

"Not particularly; I just want the opportunity to talk to you. You make me curious."

"How is that my problem?"

His eyes squint at me. Instead of pissing him off, I find amusement on his face. The smirk on his face nuzzles its way into my gut.

"Is Josh Lorenzo a close friend of yours?"

"I don't know him."

"Wasn't that you with him this morning?"

"Nope. You must be mistaken."

I pull my knees up to my chest and watch the crowd on the other side of the open field.

"See, here's the thing. I know I'm not mistaken, and I also know something was amiss that my two health inspectors were ignorant of."

My heart stops beating as I think about what I'm being asked.

He thinks the rations I took are Josh's. I so effortlessly used the rations to save some stomach growls for people I do not even know on the Outside. The same rations that may have put a target on Josh's head.

"I'm sure you're mistaken," I say and fix my eyes on the crowd at the other end of the park.

"I want to know how well you know him. Then you're free to go."

"I don't know him."

I stand and walk away, not waiting for his permission.

"I saw Meredith today. She says you and Tommy are becoming great friends."

My mom smiles as she talks, her eyes lighting up with each syllable.

"We are. More so, actually. I love him, Ma. I really, really love him." I say.

"Is that so?"

I nod my head in response.

"As long as he makes your heart happy, my dear. It's important to always be around the people who uplift you in the world."

"Does Papa make your heart happy?"

"Yes, darling. More than I could ever explain."

Chapter 3

New vegetation must be reported to assigned government

regions.

The next note from Maddox comes a week later, hidden under the fourth fence post at the southwest corner of town. Deeply secluded, and empty of everything but isolation, only debris and remnants of the corroded past liter the ground. That and of course, a perfect place for correspondence. Vitamin packets are the only words written on the crumpled piece of paper. Not something easy like food rations or clothing but damn vitamin packets. How the hell am I going to get extra vitamins?

Vitamin packets are something I actually have to use. I can starve myself or eat at public kitchens and save up food ration packages. I am supposed to turn in unused rations, but who in their right mind would do something so stupid? Vitamins show up in my blood, though. Dr. Hammid and anybody else who monitors my every move would know the instant I stopped taking them.

I could ask Josh, but he would know what I was up to, and I would never hear the end of it. Leave it to Maddox to ask for something impossible. No wonder he and Tommy got along so well.

The wind is cold and blustering. And I hate it. I tear up the tiny piece of paper and push the traitorous note into my mouth.

I pass the cemetery wall on my way home, not being able to help myself every time I come near it. I walk over to Tommy's name etched into the giant rock. My eyes locate his name amongst the thousand others instantaneously. But unlike everyone else's, his name is written with chalk, barely visible to anyone who does not know it's there. I had to scratch his name in myself after the government refused to put his name on the wall. After Frank, Tommy's father refused. I put his name underneath my parents. My entire family. All are located in the breadth of one palm print.

Every single one of their deaths is the government's fault. Maybe even Frank's fault.

I clean the dirt off their names. How different my life would have turned out if my parents never got sick. Maybe Josh would still be in Zone Four. Perhaps my father would have seen Frank for the ruthless man he truly is. But too many maybes tend to make me go mad. My shrink always says the maybes are my biggest problem. Maybe she is wrong.

The names are here as a reminder. Thousands of them. The granite monument with Frank's words engraved in the middle: *May water not be wasted. Fuel the healthy. Survive those wishing to perish our endeavors.* I hold up my middle finger to the phrase as I lay down next to the wall.

The dead grass around me prickles my skin. I run my hand through the brush and find only dirt. No grass. No plants. Not even a simple seedling. But there is never any life here. Dirt has never been anything more than dirt.

The chill in the air hits me, and I wish I had more than just a sweatshirt. Instinctively, I look for another note. But I haven't found one in this location for years. This spot has been dried out since Tommy left. But I owe it to him to look, just in case. One day, someone else may need me just as much as they needed him.

"What is it you are looking for?"

My pulse jumps as the enforcement cop stands over me, blocking my view of the always gray sky.

"Privacy."

Pushing my weight onto my calves, I knee my way back into a stance. I dust off my hands and leave handprints of dirt on my pants. "I'm not doing anything wrong."

"You're quite presumptuous, you know."

The smirk on his face bores into me, and he takes a step closer. "I was just passing through and noticed you in the dirt." He sticks his hands into his pockets and moves his eyes across the wall of names. "It is not something I typically see here."

"No. I suppose not. Mourning is not something I have seen from enforcement."

"Everybody mourns, but I've never seen anyone do it in the dirt before." He takes another small step closer to me.

"Why are you following me?"

"Believe it or not, it's incredibly coincidental."

"My ass."

"Your ass aside. Yes." He smirks as he talks, his eyes brimming with light. Seriously, no respect for the mourning.

"Well, unfortunately, I can't stick around and debate this issue any further with you. I need to be home before curfew hits. I would hate to give you another reason to suspect me of wrongdoings."

His eyebrows squint. "I don't think I ever accused you of anything."

"Goodnight, officer."

My shoulder brushes him as I walk past, holding my breath and trying to still my shaking hands.

"Kye," he says. "My name is Kye."

"I don't care."

Shivers run down my spine as I walk home. Not looking back or glancing over my shoulder, I head home and lock myself into my house.

"People need me at work, my dear. I fear without me the whole system would turn corrupt," he says.

"What does that mean?" I say.

"It means that a government needs more good people than bad. And in time, hopefully, the good rub off on the bad."

"Is Frank one of the bad?"

"No, my dear, he just hasn't found his place in the world yet. But he will. Your ma hopes it's me who is a good influence on him."

"I still wish you could stay with me."

"Me too. But when I get home tonight, we will play. Just you and me. Okay?"

"Okay. Papa. I love you."

"I love you, too, darling. Have a good day at school."

He kisses me goodbye on the forehead.

Chapter 4

All citizens are subject to random health checks. All citizens will cooperate with water enforcement officers and health inspectors to the best of their ability.

The pattern of my life continues repeating itself, on and on. Sleep. Bookshop. Breakfast with Josh. Shrink. Cemetery Wall. Feel sorry for myself. Sleep. Bookshop. Breakfast with Josh. Shrink. Cemetery Wall. Feel sorry for myself. Repeat.

Today is a bookshop day. But it is also the day I need to find my way into the injury ward and decide how the hell I'm going to get my hands on more vitamin packs.

As I shut my front door, I hear footsteps behind me. I feel the damn enforcement cop before I turn. He is everywhere I go. Stalking me in my dreams, hiding behind my closed eyelids, and now following me every turn I take. I can't escape him. His stark eyes stare into the back of my head, watching and waiting for me to slip up. Maybe even waiting to arrest me. I hate knowing his name.

The street leads me to town, but distracted, I find myself staring at the reservoir fence. Childhood memories slide past me without fail, and I stumble backward. Kye's shadow waits at the end of the fence, watching me without attempting to hide his stare. I pull on my shirt to cover the goosebumps running through my body. My hand runs through my hair, taming the dark-brown waves. Damn him. He won't even let me have the dark memories of my past.

Maybe he no longer thinks it was Josh. Why would he follow me if Josh was suspected of hoarding rations? But the idea of it makes me laugh. I am surprised Josh has not turned me in simply because it would be the right thing to do. He wouldn't do that, though. Not to me.

The weight of worry on me becomes heavy, and I turn around—screw going to the bookstore. Screw my stupid life's routine, and screw stupid enforcement. I reach the main square and find a seat on the old wooden bench directly in front of the injury ward.

Several minutes pass before the wood groans, and he sits down next to me. We sit in uncomfortable silence as I watch the doors in front of me. I watch who goes in and who goes out. I watch the slow pivot of the security cameras at the door. Kye stares at the main entrance along with me.

And I have no idea what to do. It's different when things are delivered to your door. But this? I don't know where to find stupid vitamin packs.

My impatience gets the best of me sometime later, and I snap my head toward him. "What the hell are you doing?"

He tilts his head at me and scrunches his eyebrows as if it is the only facial expression he knows. "I'm trying to figure out what *you* are doing."

I can't help but raise my voice as I jump up and stomp my foot.

"Well, stop!"

He coughs up a laugh as I stomp away, and I sense his body move off the bench. He follows behind me at a safe distance but not far enough away to relieve the tension in my shoulders.

I've been making secret drops for Maddox for over a year, and never have I ever come this close to getting caught. When Tommy did his runs for Maddox, I felt like he was under constant scrutiny. But he still got away like a sneaky fox. Every. Single. Time.

I look back every few minutes. Kye's glaze is steady on me. Even chasing me, he seems...... entertained? I get enough courage to stop when I turn onto my driveway. I spin around and face him.

Smiling at me, he tilts his head, placing both hands in his pockets. "Have a nice day, ma'am." As if he is enjoying every moment of my torment, his smile grows wider. But his eyes also soften at that moment, and he walks past my house.

I force myself not to run to the door. I bite my quivering lips as I watch him leave. He has no reason to be on this street. Three houses and an abandoned gravel road are all that lies here. It is a prison of loneliness and nothing more.

I turn and make the short trip up my driveway, but as I am about to let myself in, a shrieking cry from across the street stops me.

Three-year-old Austin clings to his mother, Lilah, as I open the front door. Lilah races towards me with the small child in her arms; his arms wrapped tightly around her neck.

His cheeks burn bright red, and tear stains streak his face. His hair lays plastered with sweat to his forehead.

Panic shines in his mother's eyes. "I need your help. I think he is dehydrated. Please. Please help us."

She pushes him at me as if I can do something. A fever is a fever.

I don't reach for him in return. I open my door and make room for her to come inside. "Put him on the couch, but you shouldn't have come here. I think I'm being watched."

She does as I ask without question. I lock the door behind her and check the windows. My stalker could not have gotten far before the shrieking began. I pull the blinds shut without thinking and take a quick reassuring breath.

Sitting next to her whimpering son, I take in their appearance. They obviously have not slept for some time. Their clothes are rumpled, and their eyes are weary.

"Is he keeping anything down?" I say.

"No. Nothing."

I fill a small bowl with water from the tap in the kitchen. I dip a washcloth in the cool water and calm my racing heart. I hate being around sick people. It never ends well. Someone always dies, and I always get blamed for it. But Austin is only three. How can I let him suffer? And poor Lilah. I know how I felt when Tommy got sick, so I can only imagine how I would feel if it was my three-year-old son.

Austin is a runner, constantly running circles around his house. Occasionally, he will pause to wave hello at me, but he is typically so involved in life he does not notice me. He is way too young for that life to escape him.

I lay the wet cloths over Austin. His hair and face become wet from the cloths, and he struggles against the weight of his mother. She remains next to him with his tiny hands wrapped in her own. I wring drops of water into his mouth and moisten his lips with what is left. "How long has he been this hot?"

Silent tears fall from her face. "Hours. I can't cool him down."

"In the freezer, pull out any rations you find with lemon or onion. Soak the pieces in one of the extra cloths on the counter.

Wrap them around his feet. Both of them."

Lilah does as I ask without question. I remoisten his lips as she works, and we sit in silence until Austin stops whimpering and fades off to sleep.

I move to the kitchen and pull out some garlic I have hidden in a vase next to the kitchen window. I let the stickiness envelop my skin as I crack open the shell. These were the last of my fresh herbs, but I rub the small bulb on the little boy's sinuses anyway. Although still hot, his fever is subsiding.

"Did you learn this from the Outside?" Lilah whispers.

I pause before I speak, the memories too overwhelming. "Yes. Yes, I did."

"I know I haven't always been very neighborly since you moved here. I should have tried harder to get to know you. How long were you out there?"

"Only a few months," I say.

"Was it awful?" she whispers. "Was it unbearable?"

I get this question often, but the truth is so much more complicated for anyone to understand. "No. Coming back was awful."

I don't continue to explain my thinking. People have a hard time understanding that coming back was not my choice. That I would much rather be out there, in the open. And when I try to explain, I am always sent back to my shrink. But something is different about Lilah. Although we've never talked much; she seems like a woman who might understand. Not that I would risk it, of course. We will never have that conversation.

"You need to stay here tonight. I'll get you blankets and pillows, but you can't leave with him until he looks better. If they see him like this, they will take him for sure. Honestly, it's a miracle they didn't see you come in. Put fresh, cold onion on his feet whenever they become warm. It's useless if it's not cold. Squeeze the lemon into his mouth once he wakes. And make sure he stays inclined like this. If it's a stomach virus, he shouldn't lie flat."

"Do you think it is? A virus?" she says.

"I hope so. You should, too. Anything else, and there's nothing I can do for him. Make sure to wash your hands as often as you can. You sick, too, will be of no use to him."

"I can't risk using too much of your water. You're already doing too much."

"It's riskier for you not to wash your hands. Trust me," I say.

"Thank you. Thank you so much." A tear falls from her face.

I shut the door to my room and leave them in privacy for the night.

Although I try to get some sleep, all I can do is stare at the ceiling.

The first time I saw Austin, he was sitting on the front stoop of his house, barely old enough to walk. I remember my first thought that maybe Frank was right. Why would anyone bring a new life into this horrible world? It only took a day or two of watching him play to realize how wrong I was.

I don't know what is going on in Lilah's head. I cannot help but wonder what she is thinking or why she doesn't get off the couch or stretch her legs. And a part of me does not know why she came to me at all. I'm not helpful. I'm barely polite. She must have someone else who could help. Right?

I did try my best, though. I could not stand by and do nothing for that sweet little boy when he is sick. I would rather die than allow the government to take one more person from this world. Especially a child.

Although the fever breaks through the night, he remains asleep much of the next day. Maybe she is too scared to leave, or perhaps my company reassures her of hope. Perhaps she can't take all the responsibility by herself. Regardless of the reason, her decision to stay unnerves me, and I can't help but stew over who to blame while her child lies helpless on my couch. The sick can be helped if only the government were to allow it. Healing instead of condemning. Caring, instead of shutting out.

She sings lullabies throughout the next day, caresses her sick child, and refuses the rations I offer her. I stay home, too fearful of leaving. I hope, for her sake, he continues to heal. No one should have to suffer loss because of sickness as much as I. Aside from Josh, everyone I have ever cared about has died due to one kind of illness or another.

"How can I ever repay you?" she says.

"Don't be silly. Anyone with an ounce of decency would have done what they could."

"No, Sara. They wouldn't. And they haven't. Years and years have gone by with no help to us. No help to anyone. What can I do to repay you?"

My eyes recognize the truth in her eyes. "I could really use a few extra vitamin packs. But I know that is a lot to ask," I say.

"Nonsense. Consider it done."

Health inspectors knock on the door the third day. My suspicions automatically verified. That dirty cop did see Lilah bring Austin to my door. They must have known he was here the whole time. But then why did they wait three whole days? Why didn't they come for him right away?

I don't recognize any of the health inspectors that come, and all I can do is hold my breath as they demand entry into my home. My heart hammers in my chest, looking at poor Austin's lethargic body curled up in a ball in the couch corner.

Lilah is near hysterics. I squeeze her hand so tight my nails tear tiny holes into her skin. But it is the only thing I can do to help keep her together. To keep her in place and her sobs at bay while the health inspectors poke and prod at her child.

But Austin's swab is clean, and enforcement is forced to walk away empty-handed.

"Sara, this is your room. Right here next to Tommy's. If you need anything, you just holler, and I'm sure he will help you, okay?"

My eyes wander from the small room up to the beautiful woman standing in front of me.

"When will my mom and dad come to get me?"

"Honey, I thought we talked about this. You're going to be living here now. We are your family."

She bends down and holds her gaze level with mine. Tenderly taking my hands, her lips try to hide a sorrowful quiver.

"Why? Is it for the water?"

The sadness deepens in her brown eyes, making a worry that I don't quite understand seem even more painful.

"Oh, no, honey, not at all. It's what your parents would have wanted. We took you in because we loved them. And you, too. We love you very much."

"We all do, Sara. We all love you."

The small boy standing at the end of the hall moves closer and takes my hand from his mother. "Let us keep on loving you, okay?" Tommy squeezes my hand ever so slightly and grins at me with concern spilling out of his eyes.

"Okay," I say, letting Tommy lead me into my new room.

Chapter 5

The United Regions federal government has the right to

regulate navigable waterways as an extension of

Water Systems Inc.

Meeting Josh for breakfast the next day brings me the same uneasy feelings. I can't see Kye following me, but I know he is there. Somewhere. A deep, dark part of me even hopes he is. Of course, I don't know why, but his eyes burn into my thoughts. Of course, I don't know why thinking about him makes me sick. Nervous even. My life is already too fragile, battling my inner thoughts each time I close my eyes. But now, even when my eyes are open, I feel trapped.

"Ever get the feeling you are being watched?" I say.

"Is it a feeling, or do you really think you are being watched?" Josh says.

"I'm pretty sure it's actually happening. But maybe everyone feels this way? Maybe there is just too much at stake."

"Enforcement?"

"That cop from the other morning. The one who came over when the health inspectors were here. Am I in for it? Do you think I've done us both in?"

"No. No, I don't think so. But you should stop being stupid. And I mean it. Stop being stupid." He glares at me. "I feel like I've been followed all day today, too. I don't think it's about you, though. I think they are after me."

"That is ridiculous. You haven't done anything wrong. Ever."

But something in his face tells me otherwise. Like a hidden secret he is not quite prepared to share.

Josh is the kind of person who behaves when no one is watching. He pays his bills on time, shows up for work early, and even helps little old ladies cross the street. He is the exact opposite of me. But something in his behavior lately tells me maybe I am wrong. I see glimpses of it in the look behind his eyes or in the way he opens his mouth after a conversation, just slightly, as if he wants to tell me a little more but doesn't quite know how.

"You give me too much credit." He runs his fingers through his hair and stares down the street. "A few years ago, back in Zone Four, I got into a pretty nasty fight with someone at a thirst station. The guy's face was messed up. I probably would have killed him if enforcement cops hadn't pulled me off him. I was put away for a few weeks." He turns his eyes to me. "Believe it or not, Frank came to my rescue." He clears his throat. "I'm worried they think I'm still involved with a few of the people I met up with back then. They pulled me in yesterday and questioned me about my loyalties."

I gaze at him and gather my thoughts. "Loyalties? What?!? What the hell are you talking about? To who? And why would you not tell me this? I always thought you were such an angel. But a fight? It sounds like you have been holding out on me."

He shrugs his shoulders.

"Tell me about this fight." I shake my head. "You know what, it doesn't even matter. You're talking crazy. I think that cop saw my bag of rations and thought it was yours. I'm sorry, Josh. If anything happens to you, it will be all my fault."

"Does that mean you've stopped your nonsense?"

"Trying to feed starving people is not nonsense," I say.

He turns away from me and stares at the street.

He can't even look at me. Annoyance? Agitation? Fear?

"You've got to stop doing it. I'm sorry, Sara," he says.

I snort. "What are you sorry for?"

His eyes catch mine, but he cannot hold my stare. He turns his head back to the street and clears his throat. "I should have told you a lot of things before now, I guess."

Squinting my eyes, I try to figure out what he hasn't said. "Like what?"

He takes a deep breath and looks at me with sadness sweeping across his features. "You and Tommy were gone, you know? With your future all figured out. Searching for freedom. A new life. A better one. I thought you would find it and live happily ever after. I guess I was trying to figure things out on my own. You two had it nailed, and I didn't. I wasn't even close. And I didn't even have the decency to say goodbye. It ate me alive."

He leans into the table, closer to me, gauging my reaction with his eyes. "Things changed so quickly. In an instant, your life shattered in pieces, and Tommy was just... ...gone." He stops and takes a few more breaths.

I wait, motionless.

"And then, all of a sudden, I had a purpose. You were back, undoubtedly against your will, locked up and refusing to get out of bed. And then I had this dream." He sits up straighter in his seat. "Tommy told me that you needed me. So, I came. If he knew I was letting you shrivel up and let go of all hope, he would haunt me till there was nothing left."

"Tommy said I needed you? You mean dead Tommy came to you in a dream and asked you to come back to this Godforsaken town to look after me?"

"Don't make it sound ridiculous," he says. "You aren't the only one with feelings."

"Tommy knew I could take care of myself."

"But you were doing a crappy job of it. Even in a grave, he could see that."

Josh did not like it here any more than I did, but I never imagined I was the reason he stayed. I remember how hard it was on me. Devastated. Lost. I felt so guilty nothing happened to me the night Tommy's life was lost. I was trying to deal with my grief. I ended up furious at the man who turned on his own son even after death. I was so angry at Frank for making Enforcement allow me back into the clean zones. He convinced them that Tommy brainwashed me and that I left without a will of my own. He said I was mentally incapable of taking care of myself.

The next thing I knew, Josh showed up and helped me put on my shoes. He got me out of lock-up. He pushed me to start living again. After some time, I began speaking. Josh is the reason I became me again. Or at least what is left of me.

"Whatever. You don't need to believe me," he mumbles.

"Don't be stupid. I didn't say I don't believe you."

"Whatever. I need to go. Just don't do anything else stupid today." In haste, he stands up and pushes like a traumatized five-year-old in his chair.

There is nothing left to say. He did not answer any of the questions in my head, and it's obvious he does not want to talk anymore. For now, I have enough to think about. Enough to feel. I nod my head at him and purse my lips together, unsure how to change the subject from here, not quite sure how to respond because I can't help but feel guilty. Is he still living here, in a town he hates, because of me?

He moves closer to me and lightly presses his lips against my forehead. One of his hands remains on the back of my neck. "I'll see you later," he whispers, then drops some cash on the table without looking back.

I watch him swagger as he walks away and can't help but wonder the true reason he sticks around. It can't just be because of me. I know his distaste for Frank. He would always choose a town miles away from him if given a choice. We both have that in common, I guess. My choice is just no longer my own.

I'm left not knowing what to think. Josh came here for me. Back to a father he hates and back to a wall full of memories he does not want. All because Tommy asked him to in a dream.

I must make it so hard for him. I'm not pleasant to be around, and I certainly have not shown him any appreciation. Appreciation for everything he has done for me, or even holding onto life when Tommy did not get the chance. I've been given the chance, and I spend every day wishing it had been me who died instead of Tommy.

Josh's sacrifice is all I can think about as I head home until I see the small package wrapped in linen sitting in front of my door. I look around, but I do not dare open it outside. I slip into my home and take the ribbon off the linen. I know who it is from—six vitamin packs based on its contents alone. My heart fills with joy. I wish there were more good people in the world like Lilah. If only

I could find a few more.

"It's okay to be sad, you know. You can cry for as long as you want. They are worth every tear you ever have, so you don't need to hide them. But if you don't want people to know, that's okay, too. I promise not to tell anyone."

I turn my face to the side, trying to wipe the wet off my face onto the pillow. I move my body to the side and look up at the boy who sits next to me.

"My dad always came in after my mom tucked me into bed. He would sneak me a kiss and wish me sweet dreams. Your dad doesn't say goodnight to anyone." I wipe the remaining tears off my hands with my palms.

"No, no, he doesn't. I think it's hard for him to feel things. But my mom does. She makes up for it. Tomorrow when she tucks you into bed, ask her to sing to you. She won't stop until you close your eyes. To me, that's better than my dad saying goodnight. It's better than him saying anything at all, actually. It might not be the same as what you're used to, but it's still pretty amazing."

"I miss them, Tommy."

"I know you do, Sara. I know."

I close my eyes and fall asleep before he leaves the room.

Chapter 6

"Excuse me, I am a little embarrassed, but I don't know where else to go."

I stand at the front desk of the injury ward, my eyes cast down, my fingers fidgeting with the hem of my shirt. "You see, I lost my vitamin packs, and I don't know how to get a new supply."

The secretary looks at me with cold, uncaring eyes. "I can give you a three-day supply. Then you need to fill out the paperwork for a new delivery." She hands me a clipboard with a pen and paper. "You will be docked a day's worth of water."

"What? That's ridiculous! Why?"

"Simple human responsibility. We can't give and take for nothing."

Her eyebrows cock at me, threatening me to verbally condemn the outlandish rules of the whole damn system.

I ponder my choices. I used so much water on Austin this week; I have no idea how much I actually have left. But then again, what is one day's worth of water? I mean, I could work all day and spend every minute possible at the bookstore. Unless, of course, there was a lockdown. Or I got sick. Or if Austin got sick again. I don't even know where these damn vitamins will be going.

"Forget it. I'll take my chances."

I drop the clipboard back on her desk and turn to leave.

My favorite stalker is blocking the door to my exit. He is smirking at me, his eyes knowing. He wipes his brown hair as it falls into his eyes. The blue-collar shirt sticks to his chest, showing off his muscular frame.

I freeze. I know I must look crazy as I look at him motionless.

He stares at me with those blue eyes that send chills over my entire body. Crazy or not, I make a decision as I walk towards him and push aside to get through the front door. I'm worried I am going to get myself killed. But I don't stop.

He takes a step to the side and blocks my exit.

"Uh, get out of my way," I say.

"No. I'm not going to do that."

"Look, you made a mistake. They weren't Josh's rations. They were mine."

"Um… what?"

His eyes never sway as he stares into me, reading me, trying to figure out what I'm doing, why I am here. "What are you talking about?" His voice hushes to a whisper.

"The rations. The rations I was hiding. I know you saw them.

They were mine, not Josh's."

I push past him and walk the remaining feet separating us from the bench outside. I slide onto the wooden bench and cross my arms over my chest, daring him to join me.

His grin fades as he walks the few feet to meet my challenge. He checks the park for onlookers and tilts his head near mine. "Um. No. If you have a death wish, walk yourself down to the station and confess, or shut the hell up."

I am momentarily dumbfounded. Why else would he be following me? Following Josh?

"You haven't been following me today?" I say.

"No. No, I haven't." He actually has the nerve to smile. "Not today at least."

My insides are shaking so much I am worried that he can hear it in my voice. What the hell did I just do? How am I going to get out of this? "Why?" I say. "Why were you following me?"

"It's my job. You get a kick out of me following you?"

"Go to hell." I stand up to leave.

His hand grabs my wrist, sending a tingle down my spine. I whip my head back to him, with his hand still holding onto my wrist. All he does is stare me down, the same smile plastered on his face.

"Tell me why you've been following me," I say again.

"I'm off today, and I'm honestly not in any mood to work. How about we hound each other a different way, like head down the street to Murphy's Café and get ourselves a drink?"

"Together?" I say.

"Yes. Together."

"You're mad. Absolutely not."

Fear glues my feet to the cement. After confessing to an

enforcement cop I had been stealing rations, I am terrified of what my next move should be. If I piss him off, I could be pulled in right now. Does that mean my confession can become a simple misunderstanding if I play into his ego?

I pull my arm away from his and sit down. "Why aren't you arresting me after what I just told you?"

"Come out with me tomorrow?" he says.

"What? No."

"I'll pick you up at six."

I jerk myself farther away from the bench and glare at him. "I said no."

"No need to give me directions. I think I'll be able to find you just fine." He smirks at me through the side of his mouth. A dimple quietly forms on his cheek.

"I said no."

I turn and rush down the street.

"Meredith, will you sing to me? Tommy said you have a voice more beautiful than any bird that ever lived," I say.

"Oh, he did, did he?"

I nod.

"Do you think it will help you sleep?" she says.

"I hope so. Tommy said it might."

She smiles at me, and her notes fill the room like the oxygen in my chest. She was rising and falling over and over again with a melody soft and slow.

Her singing makes me think of how my mother always talked about the ocean. The blue reflects off the sunsets in the sky and the rise and fall of the waves. I imagine it warm, with sand nestled in between my toes.

When her lullaby ends, I ask, "Do you miss her, too?"

The smile she gives me is sad. "Every day. Every single day. She made my heart very, very happy."

Chapter 7

Citizen curfews will be followed based on local government guidelines.

When I hear the knock at my door, I can't help but hold my breath. I stand from the couch and stare at the door, hoping I have it wrong, and it's not who I think it is. My instincts are screaming to pretend I did not hear the knock and crawl back onto the couch, but the knock vibrates again against the door. My feet are like a magnet, my mind wishing them to stop moving. I crack open the door to see who is there.

He is freshly shaven, with a pressed shirt tucked into his khakis.

"What do you want?" I say.

"I bought us tickets to the show tonight," he says.

"What part of no did you not understand?"

He reaches out his palm and pushes the door open, inching closer to me. "I brought you something." Pulling his other hand out of his pocket, he hands me three vitamin packs.

I am hesitant to take them. "Why are you giving me these?"

"I couldn't help but overhear you earlier. I know you are in need of them."

I reach out my hand and pull them from his grasp. He has left me speechless. Almost. "I'm still not going out with you."

"Would you feel better if I blackmailed you? Then you wouldn't have to feel so guilty about being attracted to me."

"Wait, what? I'm not… and no. You wouldn't do that!"

"I might actually because I really want to go to the show tonight, and I really want you to go with me."

He walks past me across my doorframe, inviting himself into my home. Uninvited.

"Please get out of my house."

"Please go to the movies with me."

I cross my arms over my chest. "No."

"Fine, if you change your mind, I'll be down at enforcement headquarters. It seems as though I have some very juicy information to report." He heads back to the front door.

All I can do is stare at him, my heart sinking. Just when I think the world can't get any darker. Bastard. "Fine."

"Really?"

A smile spreads across his face, and that stupid, damn dimple shows up on his left cheek.

I don't bother changing. I put the vitamin packs down on the counter and slam the door shut behind me. I stomp down the street. I feel his stare on me and curse him over and over again in my head. How dare he! Even if he were to blackmail me. So what? I should turn around and go home. Nothing good will come of this.

At least a theater means the small talk will be limited. It means I have two hours to calm down my resentment and feel more comfortable in my skin. Then I can avoid this happening again. I hope.

The old theater is located a few blocks from my house. Built about three hundred years ago, the shingles barely hang on enough to keep out the wind. I follow him into the lit room with red velvet seats and the large screen opposite the entrance. Concrete pillars reach to the ceiling, circling and twisting as they rise. The musty smell is palpable but made bearable by the fresh breeze streaming in through the opened windows.

I pause at the front of the theater and watch him walk up a few steps looking for a spot to sit. I can't help but think of the last time I was in a theater. Josh brought me to some show about a man dressed as a bat, just after Tommy died. I had a panic attack before the show even started, and he had to carry me out.

Kye breaks into my memory and motions to two seats about a quarter of the way up from the giant screen. "How's this?"

I roll my eyes at him as we sit down. "Whatever."

Next to each other, I don't know how to behave appropriately. What do I say, or where do I look? What the hell do I do with my hands?

He taps his foot against the chair in front of him.

I'm amused that he is nervous or feels the same way as me. I almost feel better knowing that his emotions match mine. Maybe he isn't as pissed off as me, but he has to know deep down that I don't want to be here with him. What the hell are we doing? Why are we even here? Why would he want my company when I so obviously don't want his?

"So, are you going to tell me why you've been following me, or is your blackmailing scheme too thick on your mind?" My question comes out as a stutter.

His foot stops tapping as he turns to me. The smile on his face is enthusiastic. He drops his head slightly. "No. I'm off duty."

"Bullshit," I say.

His gaze reaches up to mine, and my traitorous heart accidentally flutters. Maybe it is the unknown. Perhaps because I find amusement in pissing off those around me. Then again, perhaps it is the sharpness of his eyes. "Fine. Whatever."

He pauses as if gathering his thoughts before he answers the question. "I like you."

"Are you twelve? Please, stop yourself."

Rolling my eyes, I shift in my seat, my annoyance with him clear in my heavy sigh. "Do you typically blackmail people you like?"

He lets out a laugh that comes from his chest. "No. You're the first."

I don't know why, but something about his response makes my chest soften like a balloon that isn't about to pop but ready to release just a little bit of air.

His eyes stare blankly at the screen, his thumbs twisting and turning around each other. "You have this way about you. Like your eyes are lost, but your efforts to hide it tell of something entirely different." He turns his head to me. "I look at you dumbfounded and try so hard to figure you out. Most of it may be curiosity, trying to figure out what you're looking for. Another part of me wonders if maybe you're looking for someone to help you see what is right in front of you." He turns his head to the screen and interlocks his fingers on his lap.

"I've been looking for you, you idiot, because you are like a stalker. Always there," I say.

He ignores my comment. "But the more I watched you, the more I decided you're not letting yourself be happy, and I wanted to know why." His eyes lock onto mine showing a bit more courage.

"You sound like a creep. You know that, right?"

"If you ask my captain, it's all about the job. I follow you because of Joshua Lorenzo."

"So, which is it? Josh or your mad devotion to a girl you have been creeping out?"

"Mad devotion, huh? Neither. I don't think it's nearly as creepy as you think."

"First of all, it's super creepy." I take a breath of courage. "And secondly, it wasn't Josh. I've told you that before."

"And I'm telling you, it's not because of the rations." He leans his back into the velvet seat.

"Then what's it about?"

He flips his head towards me once more, a crooked smile plastered on his face. "I don't talk business when I'm off."

"You're an ass."

"And yet you're still here with me."

An embarrassed grumble escapes my lips at his response. I try hard to hide it, and before I can show my slip of momentary glee and ignore the irony of his words, the lights dim, signaling the start of the show, and we both relax and focus on the screen with sticky silence. I settle back into my seat, but now I feel even worse about being here. Like I am somehow deceiving Josh.

A classic I had never seen before plays on the screen. The story is about a girl with red slippers trapped in a land of magic with a wizard. I feel connected to the girl as she fights for her life to go back to the way it was. And somehow, as the movie progresses, I become more and more relaxed. Sure, Kye is enforcement. And yeah, he is a creep. But at least he is honest about both of those things. Well, parts of those things.

He puts his hand on the small of my back as we walk out of

the dusty old theater into the dark of the night. "Did you like it?"

I feel self-conscious, with only a tiny layer of cotton laying between our skin. I flinch away instinctually, and he drops his hand.

Distracted by his rashness, I have a hard time pulling my thoughts together. "I did like it, but my idea of home is slightly different than hers."

I step to the side in an attempt to shimmy farther away from his hand, just in case it decides to misbehave again.

"How so? What's home to you?"

"I think people make a home, and she had her family with her the whole time. She was just too overwhelmed with change to notice it."

"Or were the emotions just resembling home?"

Turning my body to look at him over my shoulder, I am surprised at the profound insight I haven't noticed in him before. I nod. We walk halfway down the street in silence.

I try to distract my thoughts away from him. Away from his touch. Away from the stupid-ass dimple. I hate that dimple as much as I hate knowing his name.

Kye pushes his right hand into his pocket and pulls out a red fabric badge. Without comment, he fastens it around his left bicep.

"You're kidding, right?" I say.

"No, actually. My shift started fifteen minutes ago."

I stare at my feet, refusing to move another step forward. "You are such an ass."

"To be fair, you thought that even before I put on the badge."

He pauses as I stew in silence. "So, tell me about Josh."

His voice changes, becomes sterner. Abrupt. Greedy. I had almost forgotten how I got here. Almost. I must have been so taken in by the idea of a friendship with a man that I forgot he was a crook in the government's game of life.

I don't stick around to hear anything else come out of his mouth. I know he calls my name as I storm away, but that's all I hear. What the hell was I thinking?

I cut through the lot behind the old school and push a few bikes out of my way as I head to the center of town. I wanted to go home, but that would mean circling back towards Kye. I realize my mistake too late and decided to stay on course.

It's my fault. If only I had listened to my brain in the first place. I feel so stupid. So embarrassed. I walk towards the only building that isn't abandoned, my temper rising and flaring like poison on my cheeks.

The thirst station is crowded, and I am astonished to see so many people out on a weeknight and so close to curfew. I see Josh's friends, Tony and Paul, at the back, and I am surprised to see them with a girl wearing the same mini skirt I must have had when I was eight. The same mini skirt I would never wear today.

Josh jumps over a nearby barstool and excitedly grabs my face between his palms. Visibly drunk, the uncomfortable tension that was our last conversation is nowhere to be found.

"What's wrong, why are you here? Why are you out?" he says.

"Nothing. Just because I'm out doesn't mean something is wrong."

"Um… that's bullshit but whatever. I'm so grateful you are here. Listen …" His hands drop from my cheeks. "A situation has come up, and I desperately need your help."

Josh pulls me closer to the bar and sits me down on the stool he jumped over flawlessly. "Maya kicked me out, which needless to say, leaves me homeless." He motions at the bartender and points to me.

The bartender nods and hands me a drink without hesitation.

"We close in fifteen," he says.

"You mean her obsession with you wasn't true love?" I say. "I'm shocked."

"Yeah, yeah, yeah. Anyway… I remember you telling me how comfortable your guest bed is in the house that is too big for you and you alone. What do you say?" He slurs his words as he struggles to stand upright.

"You want to move in with me?"

Careful not to let my drink go to waste, I chug it and order another before curfew hits.

"Just a few weeks. This Maya thing kind of happened unexpectedly, and I need to put some shit together before I get back on my feet. I'll take care of all the paperwork and up your water rations. You won't need to do a thing. Please?"

"Oh, please. I doubt Maya kicking you out was unexpected to anyone else here. We could have all called that one without meeting the girl." I gulp down my next drink. Drinking away worries and concerns is definitely safer than clearly thinking things through. "Of course, you can move in."

"Thank you so much, Princess. I have to go to Zone Four for a few weeks or so. But as soon as I come back, I will settle everything for you. You won't have to do a thing."

"Where will you be until then?" I say.

"I'm at Rick's. But he's heading up to Zone Four with me." He downs his drink as quickly as I did. "Thank you so much. I owe you."

"Sara! Sara! STOP! Frank! I can't deal with this anymore! Get in here and help me!"

She is frantic as she screams for her husband. Her arms squeeze against mine as she tries to stop me from dumping any more water out the window. "We need it! Sara! You must stop!"

"It will kill us! It will kill us! Why are you trying to kill me?"

My erratic screams echo across the kitchen as I try unsuccessfully to dump more water pitchers out of the house. But it flows all over the floor instead, causing us to slip. Meredith and I crash to the ground. Her screams turn into cries. She lets go of me and covers her face with her slender hands.

Tommy grabs a towel and hands it to his father, who stands motionless watching the entire scene. Tommy walks through the puddles and reaches down to my drenched body on the floor. I am soaking wet from head to toe. He takes my hand in his and helps me to my feet.

My heavy breathing begins to slow, and my eyes catch a glimpse of the chaos I have created.

"Let's go outside and talk," he says. "I think you need to calm down."

Chapter 8

All households will receive water rations based on the number of occupants.

I pace the floor as Josh brings in boxes. I'm not quite sure what it will be like living with another human being again. I have lived alone for such a long time that it's unknown to me.

He walks the boxes through the house's main entrance and veers right as the room opens up to an ample living space with an enormous stone fireplace. He already has boxes lined up by the breakfast bar, separating the living area from the kitchen. They are placed neatly next to marble countertops that no longer serve a cooking function and rustic appliances that no longer offer a function at all. All three rooms straight out to the front door are nothing but boxes.

"How does one person have so much stuff?" I say.

"I have stuff because I am actually living life. On the other hand, you live as if you were already dead."

After stacking the boxes on the bedroom floor, he heads for the couch in the living room and stares through to one of the dual master suites he now calls his own. Josh has taken the one on the east side of the house without asking. It's common knowledge that the room provides too much sunlight for my liking.

Ignoring his comment, I ask, "Is that it?"

"That's it. I really do appreciate this. I promise I won't overstay my welcome," he says.

"I'm sure you won't. But I know you'll put a damper on my self-loathing rituals."

"That's all a part of my plan. And up first is making sure this whole depression thing you've got going is just an act. I have my suspicions that it's all to keep my friend Rick off your scent."

Rick is like a mosquito. An annoying pest who lives for attention from anyone who will listen.

I sit down on the couch next to him. "Time will tell."

"I think you might be okay. I got him a job up in Zone Four."

He sprawls on the couch with his arm resting over his face, shielding his eyes from the sunlight streaming in through the windows. He reminds me so much of Tommy.

"I catch the train pretty early during the week. But if I'm ever in your way, just scream or nag at me or do whatever it is you do."

He moves his arm off his face to catch me staring at him with what I am sure is a surreal look on my face. His pose stiffens instantly, and he leans his body towards me. Memories of our childhood make my heart stop. The way he sits resembles so much of Tommy. Surely, he senses the similarity as well.

"It'll be fine… like we're kids all over again. Make yourself at home," I say.

His eyes soften as he realizes what is on my mind. "But it won't be, will it?"

The regret in his voice makes my heart falter. I don't answer his question. We both already know the answer.

Josh jumps off the couch with the spark back in his mood. "You hungry?" Moving to the giant, barely used fridge in the middle of the kitchen, he rummages through unused food rations trying to find the perfect meal to heat up.

I join him in the kitchen and check on my herbs, but they are not growing. How the hell am I going to get my hands on more garlic?

"No, I actually have to run out for a bit."

I grab a garbage bag from under the sink and head to my bathroom, where I have the vitamin packs hidden. It's still not much, but I keep telling myself it is more than they have on the outside. Besides, it's not like Maddox was very specific in his request.

I take my usual route, looking over my shoulder every few seconds, just to make sure my stalker isn't out today. I must not run into Kye. Definitely not during a drop.

My eyes gaze up at the ten-foot metal fence when I reach the northwest corner of town. It feels like forever since I found myself on the other side, crying in hysterics when I was pulled back in. I don't remember much of those first few days back inside, but I know I fought it. I fought it until I was drained of all I was and everything I used to be.

I throw the bag over the fence, and with it, I feel a heaviness in my heart that pulls me down to the ground.

The truth is, I'm nervous about living with Josh. When he isn't around, I find myself alone with my thoughts. Thoughts that pull me down deeper and deeper all the time. When Josh shows up, I battle with my insides not to pull his mood down to mine. But the opposite effect actually occurs. His optimistic attitude overcomes mine, and I laugh more than I am willing. Secretly, a part of me hates it. I don't feel like I should laugh. Don't I owe it to Tommy to be sad? Don't I owe it to myself to prove Tommy's death meant something?

I drag myself upright and head back to the house because maybe there is a silver lining. Maybe, just maybe, Josh's needs are bigger than mine. Don't I owe him to be there in his time of need, too?

But once I reach home, none of it matters anymore. Austin is sitting on my front steps, his knees up to his chin, and his mother nowhere in sight.

"Hey, little dude, where's your mom?"

He stares at me in silence, his big brown eyes expressionless.

"Does she know you're here?"

He nods his head, yes.

I look across the street to his house, but Lilah is not in sight.

"My friend, Josh, is inside. Does he know you're here?"

Austin shakes his head.

"Do you want me to take you home?"

Again, he shakes his head. "Where is Mom, Austin?"

His eyes flash down the street, but again, he says nothing.

I take his hand in mine. I can't help but relish the smallness of his little fingers in my own. I am surprised he willingly holds my hand and even more surprised when he stands beside me.

I've never had much experience with kids. None actually, aside from when Austin lay sick and lethargic on my living room couch. But he still stands with me. He still walks across the street with me, even though I am uncertain in my pace, in my grip on his hand, and how to act around a little being.

I double think my actions when we reach his front steps. The front door is ajar.

"Do you want to go in with me?" I say.

He shakes his head.

"Are you okay sitting here on the steps while I go inside?"

He nods yes.

I let go of his tiny hand and take a deep breath. He sits on the stoop and covers his face with his hands.

I have never considered myself a brave person. Even though I escaped a town surrounded by barbed wire at the mere age of sixteen, and even though I traveled by foot across the country in a land I thought would kill me, bravery was never a word I would have used. Stupid, maybe. But not brave.

But I wish I was brave, knowing that whatever I found in that house would not be something good. Nothing good ever happens in this town. Not in this life, and not to me. But what was I to do? Leave poor Austin be? Make him go home on his own?

I know what happened as soon as I entered the house. Lilah's house keys lay on the side table in the entryway. The tv is on, cartoons quietly echoing through the house. I walk into the kitchen and check the tap.

The water has been turned off. My worst fears are confirmed when I try and flip the switch by the door. The electricity has been turned off. All food rations are missing from the kitchen, as well.

My shoulders hunch, and tears fill my eyes. In a world so dark, how can things continue to grow darker?

Dragging my feet back to the front door, I pause to pick up the teddy bear hastily thrown on the floor. I sit down at Austin's side and hand him the soft brown bear. He curls his body into the stuffed animal and leans into my side.

I try my best to keep the tears from falling from my face and the quiver out of my voice. I wrap my arm around the little boy. "Austin, did the health inspectors come today? Did they take your mom?"

Nodding his head, he tries to crawl onto my lap, the bear still held tightly in his grip.

I let him snuggle onto me. His head drops onto my shoulder. "Did they know you were here?"

He shakes his head, no.

I run my fingers through his hair, quietly contemplating what to do.

I was lucky when it happened to me. I had been at school, with a plan already in place, just in case. But many kids are not so lucky. Those who are present when it happens are brought down to the enforcement office. They get twenty-four hours to be picked up by someone they know. Someone who cares. If no one comes, they are shipped to the juvenile detention center. Although they are kept separate from the troublemakers, their outlook is always poor. Putting dozens and dozens of kids together means only a matter of time before someone gets sick. All it takes is one sneeze. One cough, one case of sniffles, and a whole wing could be shut down in a matter of weeks.

"You're coming home with me, okay?"

He nods his head and stands at my side. We shuffle back to my house.

Josh is in his room by the time we get back. His door is closed and unwelcoming, which is probably for the better. The last thing we need right now is him throwing his judgments at me. But he would have to understand. Wouldn't he?

I walk Austin into my bedroom and put him in my bed. I try to remember the lullaby his mother sang to him the last time I saw her, and I do my best to sing him to sleep.

I rack my brain thinking about any other people Lilah might know. Did she have other family? Did Austin? Did they have anyone else? I do not think so. Why else would I have been the one she came to when he was sick?

I cannot let the government take him. I won't. Would it be better for him if I kept him? Give him a life with someone who cares, someone who protects him? Keep him isolated and safe from the world as much as possible? I would be able to do that, wouldn't I? Would that be the right thing to do?

Angry knocking pounds on my door minutes after Austin falls asleep. I shut my bedroom door behind me and walk to the front door. Taking a deep breath, I turn the knob.

"Hello, Ms. Carson, would you mind if we come in?"

The enforcement officer does not wait for my reply. Instead, he brushes past me, barely giving me a chance to gather my thoughts. Panic rushes over me. What if I was wrong? What if I am accused of kidnapping that poor little boy instead of trying to save his life?

The two enforcement officers stroll into my living room and start tinkering away at the frames I have on the mantel. Kye quietly walks in behind them, with his chin pulled down to his chest. The coward won't even look at me.

Josh walks out of his room before I shut the front door.

The first cop to enter the house leans against the wall behind him, with his body angled towards the second one. The name Niles is printed on the red badge adhered to his bicep. He crosses his arms as if disgusted. Kye walks in a few more feet and nods his head at me as he passes, his face stoic. He does not enter any more than need be, and he remains just a few feet from the entryway.

"What do you want, Niles?"

Josh's voice hums in the air, leaving me to think this conversation has gone on many times before. From Josh's annoyed stance, I can't help but think there is much, much more to the situation than I realize.

I shut the door, uncomfortable, even though this is my house. I feel unwelcome. As if I should not be here to witness the relationship between these men. As awkward as I feel, they demonstrate none of it. Niles pushes himself into my living room as Josh remains a statue at the wall. His stance is unwelcoming and rings with a superiority I haven't sensed around him before. Not the paternal perspective he often showers over me, but aggressive. He reminds me of Frank, not the Josh I know so well. I remain in my spot. If they would rather me not be here, they can take their conversation elsewhere.

Niles stops touching my things and helps himself to a seat on my couch, his back now turned to Josh. "Your friend Rick got a job at Water Systems. Up in Zone Four. Took over for Janson."

"Yeah, he sure did. Is there a problem with that?" Josh's voice is smooth and cold.

Niles picks at the dirt under his fingernails. "Nope. Not a problem at all. Except, of course, the transition into his new position was flawless. Only a week of training, from what I hear."

"That's because I trained him. But you already knew that, so I'm not sure why you consider a flawless transition a problem."

"You're not as capable as you think, Lorenzo. I'm sure putting one of your friends in that position was intentional, but I also think it will backfire on you sooner or later. And when that happens, you're going to be begging me for mercy. I'd like you to remember that."

Kye clears his throat from across the room. The way he digs his eyes into Niles makes me think his presence here may be vital to keep Niles from saying or doing something he shouldn't.

From what his arm badge reads, the third enforcement cop, Gage, moves closer to the mantel. He almost looks bored.

"Is that a threat?"

Josh's voice sounds intrigued.

"Oh, I don't threaten. I dig through holes and make predictions."

"What do you want, Niles?" Josh says.

"I was hoping to ask Ms. Carson a few questions. Do you mind, Ms. Carson?"

Moving closer to Niles, Josh interjects. "Sara has nothing to do with this, so leave her out of it."

Kye breaks his silence. "This will just take a minute, and it would be extremely helpful to have her perspective on things."

"Extremely helpful? To what? The made-up case you fools are trying to solve? I think I liked it better when enforcement just arrested people on suspicion. It saved a whole lot of time and headaches."

"Honestly, I don't know anything. I have no idea what this is even about," I say.

Josh's voice begins to rise. "I'm so sick and tired of this. You're blind, and you know it. Walk away."

"That's fine. We have no problem talking to Ms. Carson when you aren't around." Kye moves closer to Josh. "As a matter of fact, I am quite knowledgeable about her schedule."

Josh lunges at him, cocking his right arm back to strike Kye square in the face.

I intercede without thinking and jump in front of Kye. With both hands and every muscle in my body, I push off Josh's chest. He stumbles backward, just enough to get some sense back. Shocked. He turns and heads straight for the kitchen, rolling his neck and shaking his right hand as if he had actually made the swing.

"Get the hell out of my house," I say to Kye.

"It was nice to meet you, Ms. Carson. I would say thanks for the beverage, except you never offered me one." Niles stands up and walks towards the door. "Have a nice day." He lets himself out, and I turn back to Josh.

Kye follows Niles and Gage out the door without looking twice at me. A part of my heart crumbles as my anger towards him grows. Josh walks back to his room and slams the door without saying a word.

I find myself standing in the entryway by myself. For most of my life, I have preferred short conversations. Tommy knew I would rather be by myself or alone with him than be around others where there would be too much chatter about things that have no real value. I loved that about him. But at this very moment, as I stand glued to the hardwood floor, I want more. I want to understand what has been going on around me. This no longer feels like an issue over spilled rations.

I take a deep breath and try to steady my thoughts.

Austin opens my bedroom door and peeks out, fear in his eyes.

"Did we wake you?" I say.

He nods his head.

"I'm sorry. Don't be afraid. They're gone."

Josh walks out of his room. He pauses as he notices me and then Austin. He acts like he did not just try to attack an enforcement cop. "What now? What am I missing?"

"This is Austin," I say. "He and his mom lived across the street. He is going to be staying here with me now."

Josh is speechless for several minutes. But something about the way Austin looks at him must penetrate his soul because his body softens. He walks over to the little boy hovering in my door and kneels to his level.

"It's nice to meet you," he says and offers a handshake.

"What happened to your parents isn't going to happen to us. It was not the water that made them sick. No one is trying to kill you, Sara. We're trying to

keep you alive. The water we get is safe."

Tommy is stern as he lectures me on my bad behavior. I don't say anything as he walks me to the outskirts of town.

"But how do you know?" My voice is angry as I try and keep the tears away.

"Well, for one thing, the government tells us it is. And they are mean about it. They wouldn't be so mean if the water wasn't precious. And there are some things in life we need to trust. We need to trust that whatever happens is meant to happen. I know it's a crummy thing to say, but it's true. You're here with us now for a reason. We won't let anything happen to you."

My wary eyes look over at him. The sun rickshaws off his hair, making it look redder than it really is.

His bright green eyes read into mine. "I tell you what. I'll make a deal with you. You stop throwing water out, and I promise to always take the first sip. Anything placed in front of you, I will try it first. You'll know it's okay when you see me swallow it with no sour taste in my mouth. It'll be a secret between you and me. No one ever has to know."

I think about it for a moment and can't find any reason to distrust the sincerity in his voice. "Okay, Tommy. I'll trust you." I grab his hand and smile.

He pulls me closer and hugs me. We turn and head back to the house together.

Chapter 9

All businesses will receive water rations based on productivity or net worth.

The bookshop I own is on the outskirts of Zone Three. And by own, I mean through default. It was my mother's bookshop, part of my inheritance. Technically speaking, Frank holds wardship over the store until I reach legal ownership age, but I doubt he remembers the shop exists.

The bookshop is kind of a joke to the town. Books are a thing of the past and do not resonate much with the times. A new book has not been printed in seventy-five years. But my mother started a rental system with the books that kept the business going longer than anyone expected.

School kids are the biggest customers. They have a large chunk of time to congregate at the store between the school bell and chore assignments. The kids want to learn more about the past, unlike those who have lived it, who rarely want to be reminded of it all over again. Books seem to do that to people.

Austin holds my hand as I exit the house and head for the shop. He is fully prepared to spend the day with me. My stride remains slow to keep up with his tiny pace, but the grip on his hand reminds me that he needs me. No matter how much my life is forced to change by taking him in, it's worth it if his life has a chance.

A figure walks up my drive, dribbling a basketball. He stops a few yards from us but continues dribbling the ball.

"Hey."

"What do you want, Kye?"

My posture remains stiff, protective. Austin angles his body and tries to hide behind my legs.

Kye is wearing jeans with a long sleeve tee pushed up to the elbows. The disorder of his hair implies he is off the clock, but I've been wrong about him before. I would hate to make the same mistake twice.

"It's my day off. And you've been on my mind. I couldn't keep away any longer."

"How did you know where I lived? Oh wait, I forgot, you've already been here."

He offers the ball to Austin.

I grab the ball and hold it on my hip, my insides fuming. He winks at Austin and catches the ball back from me. He dribbles it as soon as he takes it from my hands. He bends down to Austin's level and slows his dribble, intentionally showing him how it is done.

He smirks as he stands up, his arrogance emphasizing his dimples. "I have a deal for you. Let's play. If I win, I get to take you to dinner. If you win, I walk away with my head down."

He places the ball on the ground and stretches his arms over his head. Arching his back, he shows off his chest muscles and from side to side with his arms in the air.

I bend down to grab the ball off the ground and glue it to my hip once more. "No."

He turns his attention back to Austin, still hiding behind my legs. "You think it's a good deal, right? What do you say? The first to fifteen?"

He takes the ball back with a giant smile spreading across his face. Dribbling the ball around our feet, he shoots into the net tightly secured to the roof of the empty, useless garage. It spins off the rim but goes in.

Austin lets go of my legs and runs for the ball. Handing the ball to me, he nods his head and sits cross-legged on the side of the driveway.

I dribble the ball instinctively. "You think this is a good idea?" I say to Austin. "Is this what would make you happy right now?"

He nods his head.

I throw the ball up with one hand, miss the rim, and listen to the net as the ball falls through. I glance at Kye, hoping the smugness on my face reaches its target. "No deal."

Without a word, he jumps for the ball and starts taunting me. He pushes the ball off the ground repeatedly, just like my father used to when I was a kid. I try and snatch it with an embarrassing level of failure, and he makes another basket.

I grab the rebound and set about putting him in his place. After three straight steals and baskets, I feel a little proud.

But Kye lands the next fourteen baskets and extinguishes my smugness with near perfection.

"I'll pick you up at seven?"

He puts the ball between his feet as he bends over to rest his hands on his knees and catches his breath. He looks over at Austin and winks one more time.

"No. I told you, no deal."

"You accepted the deal when you threw that ball into the air."
He winks at me again as he stands up. "I'll see you tonight."

He walks down the driveway dribbling the ball the entire way.
I watch him as he walks away, not sure how I feel. Ashamed and
humiliated but also a little queasy. But in a good way, I think.

"You're an ass!"

"You shouldn't talk that way in front of children," he says as he
waves back.

"Drink up, Sara. The last thing we need is for you to be dehydrated."

*My eyes turn to Tommy. He is peeling the plastic off his paper eating tray.
Nonchalantly grabbing his cup of water, he takes a sip, then continues messing
with his tray. He looks up and winks at me.*

I smile and drink from my cup too.

Chapter 10

Baking or cooking in a private or public residence without

a permit is prohibited.

The day actually ends up relatively smooth. Although Austin still does not speak, he spent the entire day perfectly content. He flipped through books at the store. He studied the pictures and roamed up and down the aisles. He even brought me a picture book at one point, his eyes asking me to read it to him.

I had to remind myself to feed him a few times because food was not always at the frontmost part of my mind. He did not seem to care about the rations. He ate them as asked, never knowing how much those stupid rations curse my thoughts.

As soon as we get home, he falls asleep on the couch, and I can't help but think about Kye. I can't figure him out. Is there anything to figure out? Or is his smug friendliness all a part of his ruthless plan?

Josh is not home, so I leave Austin be and put on makeup for the first time in years. I hate that. I hate that a dirty cop, I barely know, could make me feel this way. Especially since he's enforcement, I hate that I am actually going out with him. But most of all, I hate that I want to.

He shows up in khakis and a button-down shirt. The dark maroon offsets the color of his eyes.

"Austin is coming with us," I say.

"Okay… can I ask who Austin is?"

"No," I say.

Leaning over the boy on the couch, my fingers brush his wispy bangs out of his face. "Austin, honey, we're going out to dinner. Why don't you wake up for a little bit, okay?"

He rubs the sleep out of his eyes with his knuckles and tries to sit up. But he is still overcome with sleep, and his body seems sluggish. "How about I carry you, okay?"

He nods.

I pick him up and place him on my right hip. His lightness surprises me, and comfort fills my heart the moment his head rests on my shoulder.

Kye's eyes reflect his confusion. "So, you aren't going to tell me about this boy, or what is going on here?"

"Nope."

I brush past him and head down the driveway with Austin in my arms.

Kye does not push to question me. He shuts the door behind him on his way out. We walk to the small Italian Kitchen just on the inside of town, adjacent to the bookstore. It's relatively empty for a Saturday night with only one other table occupied.

I put the now fully awake Austin down as his eyes wander across the restaurant. I awkwardly sit down. Kye takes my coat, and he moves to the other side of the table. I can't help but scowl at him. It's not natural. Not the way he arrogantly walked up to my door or how he pretends that Josh didn't intend to sock the daylights out of him the other day. It's not natural the way he follows people or even the way he pretends to be more valuable than everyone else in this town. Not even in the way he so casually accepts the company I brought along on our date.

The waiter comes by to order our drinks before we manage to speak a word to each other.

Kye directs his questions to Austin. "Have you ever been to a restaurant, buddy?"

Austin stares at him but does not even shake his head no.

Kye tries again. "Have you ever had anything besides food rations?"

Austin continues to stare, his big brown eyes not giving away any emotion.

"Well, maybe after exposing you to a few luxuries in life, Sara can teach you to play basketball. She was pretty good, don't you think?" He sips the water placed in front of him.

I listen to the jingle of the ice on the glass and join the conversation without thinking. "My dad taught me. I'm not sure I would be able to do Austin any favors by passing on what I know."

"I don't know about that. I bet this little guy has quite the arm."

The way he looks at Austin almost makes me feel sad for him. He is trying so hard to get approval or even a simple response from a three-year-old, only to have silence stare back at him.

"Tell me about your dad, Sara."

"No."

His eyes turn to glare at me. "Then tell me about Austin. Either way, you've got to give me something."

It's funny how people, even perfect strangers, can come to

expect so much out of you. I don't owe Kye anything. And there is absolutely no reason I *have to give him something*. But Austin scoots over and moves closer to me at that moment. He clings to my arm. I have encouraged Austin to be scared of Kye without knowing or meaning to. And although I don't trust him enough to dish out my whole life story, the last thing I want is to give Austin one more reason to distrust the world. The least I can do is give him a pleasant memory. One with real food and, I guess, civilized conversation surrounding him.

Taking a deep breath, I pull up some pleasant memories. "My dad was a judge. He hated it, but he worked hard to provide us with a better life. I remember as a kid, he used to take me to the courtroom and give me a speech about human nature. He swore that what all people needed was a chance and that if you were fair, they would abide by the law in return." I laugh a little and look down at Austin. "He had this laugh that could change a room. I loved watching him and my mom have conversations from across the house because I only had to wait a few minutes before I was bound to hear that laugh. He knew I watched them together. He would wink at me from across the room."

"What happened to him?" Kye says.

"He failed a health exam."

He slumps in his seat. "I'm sorry. That must have been rough."

"I had an excellent support team at the time."

"Is that why this little dude is here? Isn't he the one who lives across the street from you?" he says.

I don't answer. Instead, I watch Austin as he observes the entire room around him. His eyes jump from person to person. Maybe because of his age, or perhaps because he just lost everything he has ever known, he sits so still and quiet. He is definitely something special, and I will be damned if the government ruins his chance at life.

"Do you know if he has anyone else?"

Shaking my head, my eyes never move off Austin.

"You need to register him, Sara. You can't let him stay with you if you don't register him."

"I don't have any papers for him."

"Do you want me to see what I can do? See what papers I can find?" he says.

His kind words confuse me, and my focus snaps up to his. "Why would you do that?"

"Although you may see me as heartless, I would like to think I have at least a little empathy left. A lot of enforcement officers don't join for the control and brutality. Some of us, myself included, want to help people."

I watch him as he speaks, and I wait for the conversation to shift to Josh. I wait for him to push me too hard. To lie, to cheat, or manipulate me in one way or another. But he never does, and a part of me, a very tiny part, may even believe what he says. It infuriates me.

The meal comes before I have a chance to contemplate him any further. And we sit in silence at Austin's excitement over the food in front of him. Even with a meal of simple pasta and fruit, his eyes shine as I have never seen them before. It has to be something Kye notices, too.

Kye walks us home later and pauses at the same spot in the driveway where he beat me in basketball. Looking up at the rim, he smiles. Austin is asleep again, his body limp on my shoulder.

"I had a good time with you tonight. I'm really glad you took the deal." He places his hands in his pockets and awkwardly pivots in his place.

I smirk a little. "I never took your deal."

"Good night, Sara."

He turns and walks away before I unlock my door.

Tommy and I walk hand in hand over the barren hills. We reach the top of the north part of town and stare into the east. My old ranch sits lonely out in the distance. The shutters remain closed, the green whispering to me as the color fades with the sunset.

Before my father died, the ranch was far away from everything. He loved the distance separating his home from the rest of society. He said that the space gave us purpose. Seclusion reminded us of what was at stake and gave us pride in our land even if the ground was covered only in dirt.

"How do you think two people so different could have been friends?" I say.

"I don't think our dads were true friends. Definitely our moms, but not our dads. My dad was always too jealous of yours. Still is, even after he is gone. Your dad refused the biggest job the government has ever had to offer. He was kind and loving, and people listened to him. Respected him. He would have tasted the water for every single person in town and never thought twice about it. Your dad was a very good man, Sara." He pauses and turns back west. "Don't let him die in you. Don't let his hopes and dreams die in you. Don't let fear overcome everything that he taught you. Let him continue to live with every breath you take."

Chapter 11

All water will be cleaned and purified through water sys-

tems Inc. No citizens shall purify their own water.

I am frustrated by the stacks of books that remain unshelved when we walk into the shop the next day. Austin runs straight to the back of the store where the picture books are shelved and makes himself at home.

I ignore the work I should be doing, sit on the counter, and flip through an old copy of *Time* magazine with the Man of the Year on the cover. I can't help but wonder who it would be these days if the polls were still up and running. Maybe the president who decided to throw a nuclear missile at the other half of the world. Perhaps the genius who decided to throw one right back. Or maybe even the idiot who chose to quarantine the entire east, sending millions of civilians to their deaths.

The door chimes as it opens, pulling in the crisp breeze from the street.

Kye catches sight of me before I have a chance to jump off the counter and pretend to be doing something worthwhile.

"So, this is work, huh?"

"Sorry. I can't talk. I'm very busy with all these customers. I'm sure you understand."

Austin pokes his head out from behind the back shelf. Although he doesn't say anything, he brings his hand up to wave at Kye. Kye waves back with a smile.

Kye saunters over and leans against the counter at eye level with me. He rummages through the pile of books next to me and is quiet for what seems like an eternity.

"Let's do it again."

"Do what again?" I say.

"Dinner, smart ass. If you thought I was talking about a game of hoops, you are largely mistaken. I'm not lucky enough to beat you twice."

A smile slips from my lips. "I don't know, Kye. It's weird. I really don't see this being a good idea. Plus, you're enforcement. And I hate all enforcement."

"So, you agree there is a *this?*" Motioning his arms back and forth between us, he fills up the empty space with his arms.

I can't help but laugh.

"Why are you laughing at me? Is it because I'm right?"

And in that instant, the lightness of his voice makes me want to move closer to him. "You're a hypocrite, Kye. It won't work, and you know it." I glide to the other side of the counter and fumble with the magazine rack next to me.

"You're right. You're absolutely right." He keeps looking at me as if contemplating his next move. "What about lunch then?"

I laugh once more, but I force my mind to clear. "No."

"Is my job the only reason?"

"Yes. No. But it's a big reason. It makes me hate you. How can I date someone with a job I cannot respect? And let's not forget you also have a personality that tends to piss people off."

"Do you think it would bother you so much if we were wrong about Josh? My personality put aside, of course."

"You are wrong. But even if it weren't about Josh, I would still hate you."

"Okay, so let me try and make it easier for you."

He moves to the opposite side of the counter, his body heat nearly coaxing my own. "I'll quit my job."

I roll my eyes at him.

"Okay, try this… you're beautiful, intelligent, and extremely witty." He takes another step closer, forcing me to step back, toward the wall behind me. "I know you hate my job. Probably for a good reason, but I'm honestly not sure. I've hated it for a while, too." He takes another small step forward.

I look over his shoulder to check on Austin. He is too busy with the books to be paying any attention to us.

"You're lying. You can't be doing this," I whisper. My eyes glance down to the redness of his lips as he speaks.

"I should have kissed you good night yesterday." His eyes dart up to my own. Tension fills the limited space between us. He looks down to his feet and moves backward, giving me a chance to push down the claustrophobic panic in my throat.

"No," I say. But he's right. He should have kissed me. I move around him to place the magazine on the counter.

"Sara, did you know Janson Thomas?"

I recognize the name. He was the person Rick replaced for Water Systems up in Zone Four. "I thought this was a personal visit. I didn't realize you were still on the clock." My voice grows cold.

He ignores my statement. "He was found dead in his home just a few weeks ago. Killed in cold blood. Surveillance shows that the only person who ever visited him at his home was your friend, Josh." He walks around to the other side of the counter. "Sara, I want you to know that things do not look good. And I like you. I like you a lot. I don't think you know Josh as well as you think you do, and I want you to be careful. If not for yourself, then at least for Austin."

As I feel the color drain from my face, all emotion empties out of my body. "You asshole. You don't think I know him? I don't know him as well as I think? Is that what you're telling me?"

He nods his head as if in slight agreement.

"I hate to tell you, Kye, but you're the one who doesn't seem to know very much. Especially when it comes to Josh and me. And then you have the nerve to tell me to be careful with Austin? Me? The one person on earth who is trying to protect the kid? The only person trying to give him a normal life?"

"This is not a normal life, and you know it."

"You know nothing about me." I seethe.

"I know that you were found outside the clean zones three years ago. You were delusional, probably from cleaning your own water. Once in recovery, Josh was there. He had just moved back from Zone Four. You've been friends ever since."

"Hmm. Wow. I honestly thought you would be better at your job."

He stands up a little straighter.

"Go do your homework, Kye. It's time you leave."

Understanding dawns, and he tries to force a smile. He knows he has misread me, misjudged my history, or maybe even confused his facts. He dips his head in apology and purses his lips. Lips I am trying so hard not to imagine on mine —arrogant fool.

"Keep your distance, or you'll either be killed or pulled down with him." His voice is monotone.

"Get out."

He nods at me once more and walks to the store's entrance. At the last moment, he pauses with the door open. "If he didn't do it, then he knows who did. People who are innocent cooperate. He is hiding something. We just want to know what it is." He lets the door close and walks away as the jingle chimes once more.

"Tommy? Will you stay? I don't want to be alone."

"Alone? You're not that lucky. Your poor decisions have made it clear that someone will always be around to keep an eye on you."

"I don't make that many bad decisions."

"Yes, Sara. Yes, you do. But yes. Yes, I will stay. If anybody asks, it's just because I want to make sure you don't do anything stupid."

"Fine."

Chapter 12

Any domestic behaviors deemed unfit for the restoration of

the United Regions and Water Systems Inc. will

be subject to review by local enforcement offices.

I walk through the door that night, determined to find out the truth. I don't care what barriers I need to break down or what uncomfortable questions I need to ask. Today is the day. Today is the day I figure out what is really going on.

Josh comes in from the patio, eating a microwavable food ration with a fork. I put Austin down on the couch and turn on the TV for him.

"Tell me about Janson Thomas, Josh."

He takes another bite from the paper tray and throws the remnants into the sink. After several seconds of silence, he places both hands on the counter. All of his weight is pushed forward. He cocks his head up to look at me as I slowly move closer to him. "Are they getting to you?"

"Tell me."

"I met Janson when I lived in Zone Four. I was pretty messed up and got into a lot of trouble. He stepped in and did his best to clean me up. He was the one who got me the job at Water Systems. He was the one who kept me alive when Frank wanted me hung. When I came back here, he was the one who made sure the transfer went through. Janson was a good guy. A real good guy." He pauses just long enough to look up at the sullen expression on my face. "He was shot in the head a few weeks ago. The cops think I did it. I can't figure out why I haven't been hanged or officially pinned for it yet. There is something else going on, but I can't figure it out."

I move closer to him and try not to scare off his sudden openness. "Tell them they're wrong. Tell them you didn't do it."

He laughs at my simple request. "Of course, I told them I didn't do it. But Niles is convinced that because I was the last one seen with Janson, I must be the one with blood on my hands. He's probably too lazy to actually investigate. He's been following me for weeks and pulling me into the station for questioning every time I turn around. I wake up every day thinking it's my last."

"Do you know who did it, Josh?" My voice comes out as a whisper.

He whispers his own question at me instead of giving me an answer. "They *are* getting to you, aren't they?"

I feel the blood drain from my face for the second time today. "Do you know who did it?"

"Don't be fooled, Sara. You're better than that. They are using you. I've seen what's going on. He's using you."

"What if he's not? What if some of it is actually about me?"

He thinks he's won by changing the subject. Worst of all, he knows about Kye and yet never said anything to me about it.

"If it were about you, he never would have asked you what you knew. I think you know that. You need to watch your ass and be careful. Okay?"

He closes the distance between us and pulls me in for an embrace.

I'm hesitant but return the gesture.

It's the second time today someone has asked me to be careful. The second time when I don't understand what I need to be cautious of. When my mom was alive, she would warn me about clear-cut dangers, laying very specific concerns in front of me, so I understood. *If you mess with a bee, it will sting you. If you play in the mud, you will get your clothes dirty.* I can't help feeling frustrated that no one tells me that I could get a fever and die if I don't wash my hands. No one tells me if I don't watch where I am going, a car could hit me. No one tells me that if I don't go to work, I won't be able to pay my bills, and my water will be shut off. All they say is be 'careful' when there are so many things to be cautious of. If only I had a mother around to tell me how to be cautious of men.

I drop my arms from around his waist and lock myself in my room.

"Let's race. The first one to make it to the gate wins," Tommy says.

"What do I get if I win?" I say.

"What do you want?"

I wrinkle my lips as I try and think of something. "Princess. I want you to call me princess for the rest of the day."

"Okay, but if I win, you have to kiss me." His voice is serious as he makes his request.

"Fine." I get my feet ready and take a deep breath. "On your mark, get set—"

He sets off before I have a chance to finish. I'm several feet behind him. Outstretching my arms, I try to pull on his shirt to slow his pace. He laughs as he looks back. Turning his body, he attempts a slight pivot of his feet. Fumble finds him, though. He trips, and my body crashes into his. We fall to the ground, and his laughter becomes contagious. We both stumble up with dirt covering our bodies. He regains his focus faster than I do, and he resumes his race for the gate. I reach him several seconds too late, and we both bend over to catch our breath.

"You cheated," I say and move in to press my lips against his cheek.

"I sure did, Princess. Now let's go home before we're late."

Chapter 13

If citizens collect their own rainwater, the quantity must

be claimed and turned over to local government

offices.

A knock on the front door is the only thing that forces me out of bed. I feel like I have been asleep for mere minutes, but the clock on the nightstand tells me I should be embarrassed about being in bed at this time of day. I throw my hair into a fresh ponytail and rush for the door.

Austin is curled up in a blanket on the couch and watching television.

Kye stands at the door, looking apprehensive. "Hey. I was hoping you had a minute and wouldn't mind if I stopped by."

"No, I'm super busy and don't want you here."

He ignores me and walks in, passing inches in front of my face.

"Rain's coming. A seventy-two-hour lockdown is on the way. If you have anything that needs to be done, you have about three hours before house arrests start."

Everything shuts down when the rain starts. Kitchens, schools, even government jobs. Enforcement cops are the only ones allowed out to monitor and patrol the streets and make sure no one is stupid enough to break lockdown laws. "I suppose it doesn't really affect you, though, does it?"

"The trains won't be back before the rain starts tonight. I'll be escorting people home. After that, I'm not on patrol duty."

"Three hours then, huh?"

I open the closet next to the front door and grab my shoes. I also grab Austin's shoes. "What do you say we take advantage of the time we have and get out of here then?" I say.

He smiles at me and opens the front door once more. "Austin? Let's go out for a little while, okay?"

Austin jumps off the couch and grabs his shoes from me. And although I can't be sure, I think I see a smile on his face.

"I was hoping you would say that," Kye says.

We have barely walked to the main road when the trespassing alarm bell rings. The noise echoes off every building within view, a noise so loud I instinctively shield my left ear with my free hand. Austin grips my other hand tighter and stops walking, snug against my legs.

Zone Three is heavily gated with only two main entrances. The gate stands ten to fifteen feet high with barbed wire attached on all sides. Train stations have separate routes that allow the gates to move automatically up and down so they can pass between zones. The intent of the gates is clear. No one is allowed in or out without permission.

Occasionally, a struggling outsider becomes frustrated with the strict boundary laws and finds a way in. Or, of course, vice versa. They always manage to trip a wire somehow, and the entire town goes on alert trying to find the culprits and kick them out once more.

Before my parent's death, people were allowed in and out as they pleased. My dad fought hard for it. I was fifteen when Frank Lorenzo changed all of that. He decided letting people in was too hard on our water supply. He would rather watch people suffer and die than watch his precious town become overpopulated.

Kye shouts at me over the alarm. "I'm going to check it out. How about I meet you two at the thirst station in fifteen?"

I nod, to both Kye and Austin, assuring him it's okay. I lead Austin across the street to escape the noise.

Just before I open the door, two pairs of eyes pop out from behind the dumpster to the left of the building. I pause and slowly turn to make sure Kye is not watching me. I put my fingers to my lips and encourage Austin not to make a sound. As if he actually needed the reminder. We find two boys crouched and shivering behind the dumpster, not more than ten years old. Their hair is ratty, and their eye sockets dry. Their skin and bones appearance scream of starvation. My heart sobs for them. I tiptoe over and crouch down to meet them at eye level, Austin still at my side.

"Stay here. Stay hidden. I'll be back in three minutes."

I pull Austin up on my hip and run to the back door of the thirst station. I sneak my way into the back and put Austin down by the door. Grabbing a giant potato sack, I throw food rations, vitamin drinks, even a nearby stack of soap into the bag. Quietly and quickly, I take my bounty and Austin out of the exit.

Handing the bag to the tallest of the boys, I make sure they see the urgency in my eyes. "You can't stay. You will be caught and killed. Trust me when I tell you that it will be worse than anything you have faced in the Outside. Go back the same way you came. Four miles north of the main gate, there is an old gas station. A man lives there named Maddox. He will help you from there. Rain is coming. You have to go." I help both boys to their feet.

"Thank you, Miss. Thank you so much." They peek out from behind the dumpster and run towards the east.

I hope to God Maddox is still there to help them.

We reach the door to the thirst station just as Kye approaches. He squints his eyes and looks at Austin and me suspiciously. I don't tell him where we've been as we sit down inside, but I know he is wondering why we are not already seated and patiently waiting for him.

"DAMN OUTSIDERS! Call enforcement! I've been robbed!"

The owner of the thirst station storms out of the back.

Kye lets out a very loud breath and shakes his head. He glares at me. I sit in silence, waiting for his anger to subside. I resist the urge to cower. Kye's silence is the only thing that stops me from lashing out at the owner of the thirst station for his inhumane treatment of others.

The sound of two gunshots reaches us through the front door, and the alarm ceases. Kye's eyes lock on me. Austin starts to cry.

My head drops, and my shoulders slump. It takes everything inside me not to burst into tears too. I doomed those poor boys to their death. If I had ignored them or stayed out of it, maybe they would have had a chance. Maybe they would have found some other citizen to help them in a different way that wouldn't have sentenced them to their death. I may as well have been the one to pull the trigger. Guilt and sorrow fill every vein inside my body.

I pull Austin onto my lap and try my best to quiet his tears. My hand rubs circles on his back until his tears subside. "Are you ready to get to know me better, or have you decided against it?" I say to Kye with my head down. The question runs much deeper and thicker than intended.

He does not respond at first and orders two tonics instead. "I'm sure I'm going to regret it, but yes, I'm in."

"Why?" I say.

"I honestly have no idea. I would stop myself if I could."

"That isn't a very reassuring answer," I say.

"But it's the only one I've got."

We sit in silence, my mind still on the boys. I tell myself it was better for them. They were starving, desperate, and way too young. Maddox could not have cared for them for more than a few nights.

I turn my attention back to Kye. Maybe it's because he does not carry my past on his shoulders like I feel the rest of the world does. Perhaps it's because he is unaware of my past. Or maybe, it's because he is just so damn irritating, but I may actually like having him around. My shrink says my sarcasm masks a morbid sense of humor, but Kye seems to truly understand me. But what am I saying? He kills people for those stupid codes. How many people has he killed in his career to protect his precious government? How many young boys who snuck over a stupid fence died at his hands?

I'm not sure if Kye has tied me to the robbery. I'm not sure if he knows I helped those two kids. Or tried to, anyway. But I know that he let it go even after suspecting something. He took me in precisely the way I am. He could have arrested me based on suspicion alone. He could press me about Josh every time I see him, but he leaves it alone today. He could have taken Austin from me without any questions asked.

I don't quite understand him. Enforcement Officers can arrest anyone they want and enforce any consequence they want. They think Josh killed someone in cold blood, yet no arrests have been made. Why? If Kye suspects me of trying to help those two poor boys, why is he still sitting here next to me? I don't understand it.

"Attention, Attention! This is a public service announcement. Due to impending rain, a seventy-two-hour lockdown on all civilians will begin in thirty minutes. No resident will be allowed out of their homes. All schools and businesses will be closed for seventy-two hours. Chore assignments are halted. Food rations for the 72-hour lockdown will be delivered within three hours. All citizens arriving on tonight's train will be escorted home by an enforcement officer. Lockdown is mandatory. Anyone who does not obey will be immediately arrested. You must return to your home in thirty minutes."

The service announcement funnels through loudspeakers throughout town. Kye escorts us to the tip of my driveway just as the announcement reaches its conclusion. The announcement will repeat every five minutes until the thirty-minute deadline concludes.

"Thanks for walking us home. It really wasn't necessary," I say.

"No, it was a pleasure," he says. "I'm still trying to find papers on Austin, by the way, but I have yet to find any."

I expect him to stop walking as I continue on or to turn around and head in the opposite direction. Instead, he keeps walking next to me. I break the awkward silence. "Don't you need to go home and suit up? I've never seen an enforcement escort not wearing a uniform."

"One of the luxuries of being high ranking, I guess. But you're right. I will have to dig it out of my closet for tonight. I'm very happy to say my patrol days are long over."

I always hated patrols. I associate them with pointless arrests and frivolous laws. The difference between enforcement and patrol was made clear in school, but now I am unsure. Are they looking for truth, or are they looking for people to mess up? My clearest, my hardest, and my saddest memories all involve patrol pulling me away from those I've loved the most in life.

His question interrupts my thoughts. "How about I pick you up in three days and take you to dinner?"

I don't know why, but the answer seems obvious in that moment. "Okay."

Grinning, he nods and walks away.

Josh comes home four hours later, zipped head to toe in plastic contamination coverings. His escort is wearing a matching water suit. He unzips and throws his suit at the enforcement officer.

"Absolutely ridiculous!" He slams the door in the guard's face, leaving him alone in the rain.

"Bad day?" I say.

"They know damn well people won't die from being in the rain. If they were that freak'n concerned about it, they would give everyone a plastic jumpsuit and be done with it. It's absolutely ridiculous!"

His anger trails behind his raised voice. Throwing off his shoes, he slumps down on the couch and rests his head on the backrest. He throws his right arm over his eyes.

I sit on the couch next to him. "I've always done these lockdowns by myself. It will be kind of nice having company this time."

He abruptly sits up and smiles at me. "Is that positivity in your voice?"

"No."

"Where's Austin?"

"He's asleep on my bed," I say.

"Any sign of family for him?"

"No."

"Then, did you register him yet?"

"No, and don't start with me," I say and change the subject. "Just out of curiosity, Mr. Big Shot, how will the world go on without you at work for three days?"

"I set a computer control in place before I left. The system can handle a few days at a time and be fairly self-sufficient."

"So you're telling me that a computer can do your job for you? Wow. You must be pretty important."

"I wish. Unfortunately, computers can't be trusted. Someone needs to make sure they know what they're doing, don't break down or get a mind of their own."

"Why do you have to go in every day? Why can't you just go in every three days?"

"Because people are even less trustworthy and more demanding than computers. Seventy-two hours from now, I'm sure I'll have one hell of a day cleaning up a system that shouldn't be self-reliant."

"Sounds like loads of fun."

But lockdown is much, much worse. We spend the next three days staring out the window, watching bad sitcoms, playing cards, and eating chemically engineered meals that should not count as food. I spend several hours a day trying to get Austin to talk, but the task is fruitless. The rain stops after day two, but the government trusts us so much they add an extra day just for the hell of it. I'm sure the theory behind it is to give the ground time to dry. But it is still ridiculous. They know the rain isn't contaminated. It's not going to poison us or burn our skin like in the ridiculous propaganda they try to sell to us. It's just a scare tactic to make it seem like everything they do is justified.

The phone rings at noon to let Josh know an escort will pick him up early and walk him to the train station. This, of course, infuriates him to no end. It implies that his shift starts at one, so he will be pulling an all-nighter. Although I feel bad for him, having him gone means less stress and awkwardness as I get ready for dinner with Kye. I know he will disapprove. I can imagine the look on his face if he sees Kye pick me up tomorrow night.

"Did you hear Ben Carvous talking today about the ocean? He said there were birds there. Real birds. Can you imagine? Can you just imagine looking up at the sky and seeing a bird, Sara?"

"I mean, the ocean, I totally get. But what's so great about birds?"

"Birds live in the sky. Just like the water from the clouds. If birds are safe up there, that must mean the water is safe, too. I promise you, Sara, one day I will take you to a place where you don't need to worry about the water. I'm going to take you to your ocean."

"But what about school? Do you think they have school at the ocean?"

"What do we need any more school for? We know enough. That's what makes the ocean even better."

"But I'm not done learning yet."

"What do you mean you're not done learning yet? You're the smartest girl I know."

"My Ma always said that people don't enjoy reading anymore. I promised her I would learn how to enjoy it. Now that she's gone, I can't take back that promise, Tommy."

"Well then, after you finish learning how to enjoy it, I'll take you to the ocean. You can sit in the sand reading your books with your toes in the water. The fresh, clean, crisp, blue water. It will be like heaven. Heaven, Princess. Just you, me, and heaven. It will be perfect."

Chapter 14

All able citizens must complete chore duties beginning at

age fourteen.

I am surprised at how many kitchens I have never been to in this town. Several I haven't even heard of.

After a three-day house arrest, everyone finds their way out. Never in my life have I had to wait for a table in a kitchen. Even the less fortunate have found enough pennies to venture out. The family ahead of us waits timidly against the building's brick wall. They are a young couple with a small child, about four, just slightly taller than Austin. His feet are covered in grime, a sure sign he never wore shoes. His pants reach below his knees and await another growth spurt to turn them into shorts. The woman's belly protrudes with another child to clothe.

Our waiter swore it would only be a ten-minute wait, but I don't really mind. Sitting outside feels good on my skin. The air feels fresh in my lungs, and the cool breeze the night offers is somehow reassuring that the rain was here to do good. Austin sits on the bench outside the front doors, swinging his feet as if it were a game.

"What do you normally do on lockdowns, Kye?"

"Well, that's a loaded question." He watches the family nearby. "I have an office at home. Plus, an internet connection to work. So, unlike the rest of the world, I have that to hold my attention. It forces me to catch up on things that aren't usually on my priority list."

"Hmm. Internet, huh? Was that what interested you in the job in the first place?"

"No, but with all the crap loaded on the net, it's sometimes hard to filter out useful information from worthless. Did you know that people used to take pictures of their food with the sole purpose of making other people jealous?"

"No. I always thought that they had too many places to visit with cars, airplanes, and expressways to spend time staring at a screen or taking useless photos."

"I think about it all the time. People had so many freedoms to do whatever they wanted and go wherever they wanted. But the more I think about it, the angrier I get. Maybe if they had more laws and fewer freedoms, we wouldn't be a species struggling for survival."

"This is where we disagree, Kye. I think it's the government that screwed it all up for us, not the citizens," I say.

He grins a cocky grin. "So, you hate the government; you hate the water laws, you generally don't trust people, and yet here you are with me. An enforcement cop who works for the government. In a gated-up Clean Zone."

"Oh, please. I only trust one person on this planet, and I'm working hard as hell to make it two. And *he* doesn't even speak to me." I pat Austin on the head. "Although you make a good argument against trusting people, keep working at it; you have extra work to do now that I know you have a patrol uniform."

We are seated, and I can hardly handle the anticipation. After nine straight meals of pretend food in a box, my mouth salivates just looking at the menu. I decide to order an artichoke and asparagus salad with stuffed peppers dribbled in garlic sauce on the side. At first, Austin looks at the food as if it were poison, but puts it in his mouth nevertheless.

The meal is absolutely delicious, making me so happy that I actually laugh while eating. Of course, this makes Kye laugh at me, which leads to a delightful dinner. By the time we finish eating, I am so full I can barely sit up straight.

I relax and let my food digest. The small family who found their way in ahead of us has one small plate in front of the three of them that they shared. The plate is licked clean, but the little boy still looks starving.

"Can you do me a favor?" I say to Kye before thinking about what his response may be.

"Depends. Will you like me more?" he says.

"Absolutely, I will." I motion towards the small family. "I want you to pay for their meal."

He looks over at the family then back at me. "They came in knowing they would have to pay, which means they can pay for it on their own."

"I didn't say they couldn't. What I'm saying is that they look like they are struggling. And you are in the perfect position to help them." I keep my eyes glued to him as I try watch to see what kind of person he really is.

Kye takes a deep breath and stands up from the table. He heads to the waiter, busy behind the counter. The waiter stops to listen to Kye and nods in understanding. Kye hands him cash before coming back to our table. The waiter brings three more dishes to the small family several minutes later. The man tries to send the food away, but the waiter remains relentless and continues to talk to them, urging them to accept the three gifted plates.t I can see by the look in their eyes the moment the waiter informs them that the meal has been paid for. All three glance around the restaurant in shock and confusion, searching for the anonymous donor. The waiter walks away, and the family begins to eat again with smiles on their faces.

I look at Kye, who is sheepishly smiling. "Thank you," is all I can manage.

His smile overshadows the softness of his eyes, eyes I often overlook. I don't know if the kindness has been there the whole time or if it is something new, but it helps the air in the kitchen feel cleaner, safer. We sit in comfortable silence for several minutes, enjoying the moment. Austin busies himself with the silverware on the table.

"Curfew is coming; I'd better take you two home," he says.

"Ugg. I've never hated being home so much in my life." I pause as the words come out of my mouth. "All right, maybe that's not true, but I still don't want to go."

"Well then, let's walk slow."

Streetlights dimly light up the path, but the night is dark, and it empowers me. I feel as though I'm back on the outside, in the darkness of night, looking up at the sky and seeing the stars. I wish with all my heart that we were able to see the stars in Zone Three. But the pollution in big cities took away the privilege of such beauty long ago. Even though I had them for what seemed like a mere moment in time, their loss tore yet another hole in my heart.

Holes mend, though. At least, that is what I hope.

Kye takes hold of my hand as we walk up to my drive. I let him. He picks up Austin and carries him the rest of the way.

"Can I walk you in?"

I agree.

He moves closer, and we stand face to face. I don't back away.

"Where does this little guy sleep?" he says. "He is just about out."

"Couch is fine," I say.

Kye lays him on the couch and covers Austin's near-limp body with a blanket. His eyes close, and he turns his body against the couch cushions already fast asleep.

Kye approaches, a mere inch from my face. I am breathless as he glides the back of his fingertips down my cheek. I feel his body lean in closer, and I'm ready to embrace his kiss. Instead, he steps aside, clears his throat, and walks to the door.

"Wait!"

The words fly out of my mouth before I can stop myself, and I rush over to him and pull his head down to mine. Our bodies hit each other with a passion I am unprepared for. I fumble backward, and my back slams against the wall behind me. Breathing intensely, I ignore the difference between right and wrong. This is the moment I care about, the only moment that matters. His shampoo is the only thing I can smell. His lips pressed against mine are the only thing I can feel.

His hand pulls on the small of my back. My fingertips, wrapped around the hair on the back of his head, keep me from falling over faint. I guide him to my bedroom and shut the door behind us.

"Kids, we need to talk," Frank says. "They lowered the water rations. They're enforcing new codes. Starting today, we have to make a lot of changes."

We all sit on the couch staring up at him, unsure what to say. Frank lists the new codes being forced on all citizens living in Clean Zone Three.

Tommy wrinkles his brow. "It sounds like we will be prisoners, dad."

"I know it will be hard. But I also think that it's probably temporary. As soon as Water Systems gets enough backup, things will go back to how they were. Maybe even better. Bottom line, we need more piping systems." He starts pacing in front of us. "We have too many people in the Clean Zones, and we need time to get the system up and running."

His voice is calm as he tries to reassure his son. I wonder if he himself is reassured. Probably not.

"But a curfew? Activity restrictions? Government chore assignments!? Why the kids? Doesn't it sound ridiculous to you? What happens if we don't?"

Tommy's rage begins to grow, and his voice gets louder and louder. Not at his father necessarily, but about everything. Everything life has to offer that he isn't allowed.

"Punishments will depend on the crime. It might be lower water rations or an increased chore assignment if it's minor. Breaking a curfew may lead to house arrest. Increased physical activity will lead to lowered water rations. Anyone caught leaving a Clean Zone without permission may not be allowed back in."

His eyes drop, and it is obvious he can no longer look his children in the eye. He doesn't tell us the worst of the punishments, but we all know them. We've heard the stories.

"They are also shrinking the borders, fencing off the outside. There will be no more roaming around like wild animals. Say your goodbyes now, Sara, because after next month, your old family ranch will no longer be accessible."

Chapter 15

Citizens may not add or remove vegetation from public or private grounds without a permit.

I hear him getting dressed as I wake up in the morning, my mind trying to wrap itself around the events that occurred last night. I replay each moment and smile to myself even before opening my eyes. Maybe he isn't so bad after all. He did try to convince me he had somewhat of a heart. Maybe I was too closed off to see it. Maybe.

My memories come to a halt when I hear Josh making coffee in the kitchen and talking to Austin about God knows what. I roll over and open my eyes a second too late. Kye is shutting the door behind him and walking into the kitchen.

I jump out of bed with every intention of stopping them from dueling it out in my kitchen. But the second my hand hits the doorknob, I hesitate. I crack open the door and peek out to glimpse the two men in my kitchen.

"You have got to be kidding me!"

Josh puts down his coffee and shakes his head in complete disbelief. "Can't you get fired for something like this? Arrested maybe? Isn't there some ethical code you're breaking?"

Kye ignores him and walks over to the pictures on the mantel. He looks at them, one by one, and takes his time, deep in thought. His fingers brush past a frame of my parents, and he stops and picks up the fame next to it. Josh, Tommy, and I have our faces pushed together. All of us are laughing. He puts the frame down and stares at a picture of Tommy and me, my head resting on his shoulder, smiling in an embrace.

"She's had a lot of loss in her life, huh?" His tone is soft, full of genuine empathy.

"Yeah, she has. Enough heartbreak for a lifetime, *don't you think?*"

His tone is accusatory. He rests his palms on the counter, his chest rising and falling in quick succession. He is trying so hard to hold in his temper.

I can't see Austin, but I hear his tiny feet scamper across the floor into Josh's room. The door clicks shut behind him.

I take a quick breath, open my door, and slowly make my way to the coffee.

Josh's voice rises. "Sara, what the hell were you thinking?"

His face is red, and he makes me feel like a child being scolded. "Good morning to you, too." I keep walking towards the coffee, but I throw him a look of irritation.

"Please, God, tell me you weren't thinking at all!"

He pulls the coffee cup out of my hand and keeps scolding me. "He's using you! He's a dirty cop who obviously has ulterior motives! I can't believe you would be okay with this. I can't believe you are being this stupid!"

Kye remains silent in the living room and watches the scene

unfold in front of him.

My embarrassment turns to anger. "Why are you so angry? Did you ever once think that maybe not everything has to do with you?

"It has nothing to do with me? Are you freaking kidding me? I've been pulled into the station three times in the past month by this dip shit! Do you think it's a coincidence he sticks around? My God, Sara, get a freaking clue!"

"Tell me why, Josh! Stop with the bullshit and be honest for one damn second!"

His voice low and stern, his lips pursed, he points at Kye. "I'm not having this conversation with you when *he's* here. You betrayed me, and you freaking know it." He points his index finger at my chest, and I cringe like a child. "I hope it was worth it."

I can't help myself. Even if he might be right, I feel trapped. Looking him in the eye, I keep my voice steady and calm. "It was."

In one swift movement, he picks up the cup of coffee and launches it at the wall. The cup shatters, coffee flies across the room.

I jump away.

He opens the door to his room, his voice bellowing. "Austin, dude, you're coming with me today."

He storms out of the house and slams the front door behind him; Austin, silent as ever, is firm on his hip.

I rest my arms on the counter. The touch of granite helps keep me steady. My eyes are filled with tears that I refuse to let fall. I am trembling as the effort begins to overwhelm me. I know Kye is watching me, his hand cupped over his chin, fingers resting over his mouth. "I should go," he says quietly.

I nod at him, unable to say a word. My eyes meet his, and my thoughts suddenly shift. Maybe I was the one who used him. I knew all along that this could never go anywhere. I was a part of his job. I knew his intentions. I knew he wanted dirt on Josh. I knew it was a bad idea from the get-go.

"I'm sorry," I whisper.

"Me, too."

He walks over and kisses me on the forehead. The gesture is something that Josh would have done. "In all honesty, I truly had no idea. I'm sorry."

What could I say?

"I'll call you later."

He turns and walks out the same door Josh slammed moments ago.

"Dad, we promised to keep Sara safe. All these new laws and codes make it seem like we can't do that yet. If the water is safe enough to drink, why isn't it safe enough to let the people do whatever they want with it?"

"These laws are what keep you safe, Tommy. Not just Sara, but all of you. People can't be trusted. It's time you learn that." He appears annoyed as he brushes his hand across sweat on his forehead.

"Give them a chance, dad. Give us a chance." Tommy sits down on the couch and puts his hand over his forehead.

"Tommy, your ignorance about the world will be the end of me. Stop trying to be everyone's protector and follow the damn new laws." Frank glares at him as his anger turns to rage.

Tommy stands up and storms out of the room.

"It's all she has left of them."

I tiptoe out of my room to peek in on the conversation.

"I don't care what you have to do, but it's the only way I will ever speak to you again." He tears the pillow out from under Frank's head and spews his demands. "I know you had something to do with these new codes, so don't you dare bullshit me. Their old house is the only thing she has left of them. Now you tell her it's outside a clean zone, and she will never have a chance to see it

again? Figure something out, or I will tell your commander about the shrubs you're growing in the basement," Tommy says.

Silence fills the room. "Fine. I'll take care of it."

Chapter 16

Leaks in/ and around taps must be reported to Water

Systems Inc.

I leave the broken cup on the floor and go back to bed. The only way I can prevent the tears from spilling out is to get some more sleep and pretend that none of this ever happened. Pretend that it wasn't me who created such a devastating mess. Pretend that it isn't me who is falling for Kye.

I dream of Tommy. We are driving towards the field by my grandparents' house in Poway before Zone One was restructured to exclude it. We stop at the side of the road, and I wait in the car until he opens the door for me. I reach for the hand he holds out. We're walking towards the great oak in the middle of the field when I notice that I'm limping and my foot aches. "I need to stop," I say. "It hurts too much."

"You can't stop, Princess. I'm not going to let you."

He picks me up and cradles me like an infant. He carries me

the rest of the way to the tree. A blanket lay on the ground, and he gently puts me down. We lay there in silence, looking up at the sky. I have so much I want to tell him. I want to remind him of how much I love him and how much I've missed him. I want to wrap my arms around him and never let go. I want to tell him how sorry I am that I survived and he didn't.

I close my eyes for a split second and when I open them, I'm in the middle of a storm. Dead leaves are blowing against my face, and my eyes are filled with dirt. Brittle ground surrounds me. I look towards the giant farmhouse to my left and see a tornado tearing the beautiful structure apart piece by piece.

Screaming, I jump to my feet. Tommy remains flat on the ground with his hands braced behind his head. Turning his head to me, he snorts out a laugh. He starts speaking, but the wind tears his words away. He seems untouched by the destruction around him, and he brushes the wrinkles out of his shirt as he stands.

I scream at him. I reach for him as the tornado's eye creeps closer to our spot.

"Walkthrough it, Princess."

I hear the words as he is lifted out of my grasp.

I wake up in a sweat. It's hard enough to lose him once. Each time I dream of him, I feel like I'm losing him again and again.

I roll out of bed and pop a pill. Brushing my teeth, I stare at the girl in the mirror. I don't recognize the eyes. There's a darkness there that I don't want anymore. I want a light again. I want to feel good when I crawl out of bed in the morning. I want Tommy with me, not in a dream.

I prick my finger and drop the blood sample into the mailbox before I get in the shower to wash away my sorrow. I let the water run down my betrayals as well as my guilt. Several minutes too late,

I realize I'm not going to have enough water for the next two days. I get out and dress in jeans and a tank top. I dry my hair as if it weren't already eight at night. I drag myself into the kitchen and tear open a package of cereal while staring at the broken cup on the floor.

He was right. I wasn't thinking.

I put my tray in the sink. My long shower ruined all hope I had for cleaning the floor today. I stare at the glass and the dried coffee stains on the floor. I pull out the broom and attack the broken glass. I see Josh's shadow walking up the drive just as I'm finishing up. Austin is chasing the basketball around the driveway. The bounce of the ball echoes off the house.

"He's using you."

The words fly from his mouth as soon as he enters the house. He walks into the kitchen and pours himself a drink. Peppermint schnapps. A sure sign that he has been drinking all day.

"I'm sorry I hurt you. That wasn't my intention," I whisper.

He turns and in one swift motion grabs me by the hips and lifts me to a sitting position on the counter. Our eyes are even as I gaze into his. He glides both hands down the back of my neck as he moves the hair out of my face. My breath quickens. I can smell the peppermint on his breath and feel the penetrating look capturing my eyes.

"Josh, what…?"

He drops his head to rest his forehead against mine and begins to whisper. "I've never questioned your place in my life. You've always had a place. When we were kids, you were the glue that kept my family together. And because of that, I felt as if I needed to protect you from the world no matter what. I cleaned your scraped knees. I would have helped you with your homework or taught you how to get out of trouble. When you and Tommy started talking about leaving, I expected it. It was something that was meant to be." His voice catches. "When he died, I tried to help you get back on your feet as much as possible, without question. Your attitude had changed, but you were still there."

He taps his fingers against my chest, motioning to my heart. "When you started going out, I always knew you were just pretending to be moving on, that you weren't happy. You weren't even close." He pauses but keeps his hand resting on my heart. "But this morning … when I saw him walk out of your room…" He hesitates.

I hold my breath not quite knowing how to breathe this close to him, his forehead still resting against mine.

"I was jealous."

The words are unexpected. I try to pull my head back to get a clear look into his eyes. My hands reach up to his cheeks, and he immediately grabs hold of them, softly cupping them.

"One day, you're going to figure out how much I love you. And when you do, I pray that you don't feel the same about me. You can't trust people in this world, Sara. There are things out there that are too big. Misguided, transformed, and unappreciated."

I place both of my hands on his chest and push him back slightly. He clasps his hands around mine with more intensity.

"Can I trust *you*, Josh?" My voice comes out in a whisper.

He does not answer at first. We continue to breathe in each other as if the question was never asked. My pulse races. This is Josh. *My* Josh. Sliding closer to him, I ask the question again. "Can I trust you?"

He lets go of my hands, pulls my chin into his, and brushes his lips against mine.

"You need to call someone about the drip on your faucet," he says.

"Don't change the subject. Can I trust you or not?"

"No. No, you can't."

He pulls back and wipes a single tear as it falls down my cheek. He pulls my hands to his lips and kisses the back of my hand as gently as he had my lips, looks me in the eye, and walks away.

I'm left sitting on the counter. Unable to control my pulse or hold in the tears. God knows, I have tried for years now. They are silent as they fall with unkempt hopes and dreams washing away with my best friend. I walk to his room and place my hand in the middle of his closed door. Was he even in there? Had I misjudged him all along?

"Why do you think they gave us all chores?"

He turns his head to look at me as we lay under my parents freshly carved name plates.

"Probably because they don't want us having minds of our own so they need to keep us busy. I mean, think about it. I read once that the brain stops growing at the age of eighteen when chore assignments stop. Do you think that's a coincidence? They don't want us figuring out that there is a better way to do things."

He leans on his elbows and turns his body to mine. "Whatever the reason is, at least our chores are here in town. I heard that after sixteen you're pushed to the outskirts to help with clean-up duty."

My mind tries to understand what he is telling me. "Aren't they worried about kids getting sick?"

"I heard my dad saying that kids have more immunities to contaminants. Plus, I'm sure they put on contamination suits. Besides, grownups have jobs, and I guess someone has to do it. If we all do our part, then maybe things will be better when we grow up. I'd like to sit in the rain one day and let it drain into my mouth. I want to live by the ocean like I promised you. Would you still

come with me, Princess? I mean it's not a silly dream anymore. I want it to be for real. Would you come with me to the sea?"

"I'll follow you anywhere, Tommy. I promise I'll live at the ocean with you one day."

Chapter 17

Citizens who leave the safety of a Clean Zone will not be allowed back in for the safety of the zone's remaining citizens.

The next morning, Josh is gone. Austin and I walk to Ari's Kitchen thinking he is planning to meet us there, but he never shows. I end up drinking a cup of coffee by myself.

I wait for days, wondering how I could have done things differently so he stayed. I do inventory at the store. I spend hours at the cemetery. Then I do it all over again. Austin, with no choice but to follow me everywhere I go, gets more creative with his time. He colors on the sidewalk with rocks, makes a bridge out of books in the store, and attempts summersaults everywhere we go.

I can't help but wonder if I am truly doing right by him. But what other choice is there? Not one person has come looking for him. Not one.

A week goes by, and we head to Ari's Kitchen once more, and

wait for Josh. But he never shows up. I drink coffee by myself, Austin perfectly silent, always at my side.

I skip my appointment with Dr. Hammid. I know there will be hell to pay for it, but I can't convince myself to go. Especially with Austin. I would not let him near that office. Dr. Hammid would not let him leave with me. Besides, the last thing I want to do is talk. Especially about my life choices. So I don't talk at all. I hide inside my head and stare into my past. I watch as my life passes before my eyes, and I feel sick about not doing things differently. But even now, it all goes back to Tommy. I should have done things differently back then. I wish I had known so many things. Been prepared for a life outside of a clean zone.

I take Austin back to the store and try to get my mind off things. I spend some time reading to him, but he soon becomes bored with me and heads to the bridge of books he created.

I'm behind the counter counting change when the chime rings, and I catch my breath. Kye walks through the door. My heart pounds in my chest. One of the two men who abandoned me within one moon phase.

I'm not sure what to say. I want to lay my head against his chest and count the beats of his heart, but I can't. That might give him the impression I care. And I don't, do I? I want to tell him everything that has happened. I want to know why I haven't seen him for over a week. I want him to embrace me like Tommy would have, and tell me not to worry, that the rain will wash it all away. But I don't. His eyes would read mine in a matter of seconds, and he would know how awful I feel. How guilty I feel. Guilty about everything. But worst of all, I feel regret. Regret that Josh found out.

He stops at the counter and looks around. "Busy day, I see."

"This is it. Mornings tend to be rough."

I keep my hands busy with paperwork on the counter and try not to look at him.

"You're the only bookstore around for hundreds of miles, and you're telling me you don't have a steady line of customers?"

"Aside from the school kids, no, I don't. People come in here thinking it's a museum. And let's be honest, everything in here is an antique. I'm just hoping people start publishing books again before I die."

"How do you stay open? Why hasn't the government shut you down?"

"Before my parents died, they were in the habit of hiding money in their mattress. I foresee at least a few more years before I close shop. The kids help a lot though."

He smiles. "Are you telling me there's money in your mattress?"

I smile. "No, I keep it somewhere else. I'll let you know if you ever get too close to my secret stash."

He looks at me with the same small smile that caught me off guard the first time I met him. My eyes become stuck on his baby blues, and the sternness inside me softens.

"Sara, I have some bad news."

He glances to the back of the store, searching for Austin. "There are no papers. No records of his birth. Nothing." His eyes are somber as he turns to face me. "Without any registration, you can't keep him. It won't just be him at risk, but you, too."

My insides grow cold, agitated by the world I live in. "Keep him?" I say. "He's a person Kye, not an object to be bought and sold from the store."

He frowns, a sad, sympathetic gesture I try not to react to. "He can't stay with you."

Every day when I wake up, I think things can't possibly get any worse. Luck will change, I tell myself. Maybe the wind will change directions. But it never does.

I know I may not be the best choice for Austin. I've always known that. I know I don't have a clue how to raise a kid, or to feed him properly to make sure he never gets sick again, or even how to do something as simple as entertain him. But I have no other choice. "If he goes to the detention center at his age, he will die. If not through illness, then through euthanasia." I try to keep the tears out of my whispered voice. "Kye, you know this."

"If you're caught with him, you'll face charges, too."

The tears can't hold back any longer, and they slide down my cheeks. "Then don't tell anyone." I slide down the wall behind me and curl my arms around my legs. Kye sits next to me. His arms rest on top of his knees.

"It may be what happened to his mom, Sara. Have you thought about that? Maybe it wasn't a health inspection she failed. Maybe they found out and that was her punishment."

"How could you be a part of something so cruel? So inhumane?"

"I know you don't believe me, but I joined for other reasons. I joined so I could help. So I could do everything in my power to make society better. Better for all of us."

My eyes dry up at his words, and my head snaps to him. "Then go do your part. Make society better for him, and you better make damn sure he is a part of it."

But I can't stay any longer to hear what he has to say. I don't have patience for it, and I don't want to hear any of his excuses. Austin has no chance living in a detention center. None.

I rush to my feet and grab Austin, knocking over his book bridge in my haste. His face turns down in a frown, but he doesn't make a peep. His hand reaches for Kye, still sitting on the floor, his back pressed up against the shelves as if in a time out. I leave him there in my store as Austin waves goodbye.

I run with him in my arms, through the center of town, past the enforcement offices, and past the reservoir fence. At my house, I use my free hand to scribble three notes, then I run out the door, never once putting Austin down. It feels as if I am carrying a tank instead of a small, malnourished boy. A boy with barely a chance at life, and me his only hope.

I keep running and make my way to the cemetery. I stumble over rocks, and trip over my feet. Only faith keeps me upright and Austin in my arms.

He wraps both arms tight around my neck as I slow, and he crawls onto my back as I kneel in front of the stone wall in front of us. Running both my hands through the dirt, I make sure there are no other messages, and bury my first note.

I try to stand but I am overpowered by the heaviness in my chest. I drop to a knee with one hand resting on the ground to keep my balance. Austin swings his feet and shimmies off my back. He kneels next to me, and I stare him in the face.

"Sara sad?" His tiny voice brings tears.

"Yes." I hiccup. "I am very sad." My eyes soften at his sudden willingness to speak.

His tiny palm reaches out as he tries to wipe the tears off my cheeks. His arms wrap around my neck once more, and I hug his little frame.

"Go home?" he says.

"No buddy. I can't take you home. It's not safe for you there anymore." I take as many breaths as I can and try my best to calm my breathing. I pick him up once more and gather the energy to move to my second drop spot.

I only make it to one more stop. My note begging for Maddox's help is flattened under the fourth post of the ten-foot metal fence in the southwest corner of town. But once I dig the note under the post, I no longer have the energy to run. Austin stays on my chest, his legs wrapped around my waist, his arms tight around my neck. We are barely on the main road again before we run into Kye.

I stop in my tracks, terrified of which man he will choose to be.

"Please stop and listen to me."

"Please don't take him from me, Kye. Not yet. Please." My words come out in sobs. I try my best to stay calm for Austin, but I have no calmness left in my control.

"Just stop for a second and listen. I am not taking him from you."

He holds out his hand and motions for me to calm down. "I don't have a good plan. But it's the only plan I've got." He takes a few steps closer and lowers his voice. His other hand holds the crinkled dirt-ridden note I hid at the cemetery. "You once told me I wasn't very good at my job. And although you're probably right, I need your help to pull off this piss-poor plan."

I am speechless as I stare at him, as I contemplate my choices and the lost hope of the note now crinkled in his hand.

"Get us to your contact on the outside, and I promise to pay passage for Austin's way out."

My mouth drops open. It could be another trap. Another devious plan to catch me doing wrong and get me stuck on the outside with no preparation and no clue how to help Austin. But I fear I have no other choice. Austin may have no other choice.

"I want to keep him safe, too, Sara."

"You need to prove it to me. I don't care how, but I can't trust you. At least not yet." I wipe a tear from my face. "Prove to me you can keep him safe."

He escorts us to a black Jeep parked at the side of the road. "Austin." He reaches for him, gently pulling him out of my arms. "We are going for a ride."

He opens the side door and pushes the front seat forward. "But it's a secret ride, okay? For us to stay secret we have to keep you hidden under this blanket. Do you think you can do that for us?"

Nodding his head, as cooperative as always, Austin climbs into the backseat of the Jeep. Kye loosely tucks a blanket around his sides, with a small window hole for his tiny face. He remains out of sight.

Climbing in the seat beside Kye, I try to stop my tears.

I haven't ridden in a car since I was a kid. It feels as if I am floating on the wind, each breath threatening to get caught in my throat like I am drowning.

We reach the East Gate. Four-armed enforcement officers stand patrol in front of the iron steel bars. Kye drives straight to them.

Panic rises in my throat. "Kye, I can't leave. I already have one strike. They won't let me back in."

"You'll be fine. I'm allowed out any time I want. As long as you're with me they won't even ask for your papers."

He sounds so sure of himself, but I can't help my fear. I want to throw up.

"As long as they don't see Austin, of course. That would be a completely different story with a very different outcome."

My stomach ties itself in knots.

He slows the Jeep and approaches the four men guarding the roadblock. The gate stands twelve feet high and stretches around both sides of the road. Barbed wire spins at the top and then disappears into the horizon.

Kye stops at the gate and pulls out his badge to show one of the guards. Without a word, the guard motions us through, never looking twice at me, never even asking Kye his purpose or his authorization. Memories flash me back to years prior, of digging a hole under the gate in the mud, in the darkness of night. Now, two years later, we go right through it. Years ago, it was so hard for Tommy and I to get to the other side. And now I slip right out with Kye, but he is clueless to the whole memory. How difficult it was for me the first time. The idea devastates me. Why is life hard for some of us and not for all? What did I ever do to get punished with so many hardships?

The road ends a few hundred yards after the gate's entrance and becomes a bumpy trail overwhelmed by decades of neglect. Mounds of dirt and boulders make a jagged course that seems to follow what used to be a street. The farther we drive, the dryer the air becomes. We drive toward the rubble that used to be a town called Riverbend. What it was in its past has become crumbling houses with shattered windows and overgrown brush. The Jeep moves through the town's ruins, in and out of holes in the ground, and over dead fields that used to be play areas for children.

Kye stops the Jeep just outside the dead town. "Austin, you can come out now. We won't be able to go any farther in the Jeep. We need to walk from here. I want to show you two something."

I follow his directions and stay close behind him, with Austin at my side, gripping my hand with his own. I'm not sure where we are going, and the walk is rough. I crawl over fallen trees, push brittle vines out of my face, and pull thorns out of my pants as we go. I lift Austin over fallen debris and catch him each time he falls.

Kye picks him up after his foot gets stuck in a hole, and we must dig him and his little shoe out. We walk through the brush to a secluded creek, hazy with dark green water. I am out of breath by the time we get there.

"Come here and take a look."

Kye bends down with Austin and leans over the water. His grip is tight on Austin to make sure he does not topple in. He motions for me to do the same. I see the ripples in the water first. Small currents flicker in the water, then an orange tail glistens in the water.

"What is it?" I bend down to get a better look, shoulder to shoulder with Kye and Austin. The shape swims towards a pile of rocks collected near the side of the water.

Austin giggles and covers his mouth with his free hand. The other hand stays tightly gripped around Kye's neck.

"What do you mean, what is it? It's a fish."

"I've never seen a live fish." My voice is a shocked whisper. "How did it get here?"

"I'm not quite sure. It probably swam in from a larger body of water. But if there is *one* there will be more."

He sets Austin on his feet and sits down.

Austin inches closer to the water. He kneels as close as he can and points to the fish with a smile on his face.

"What does it mean?" I whisper.

"I wouldn't trust it enough to drink the water or eat the fish, but it definitely points to nature cleaning itself up."

Grabbing a nearby stick, Austin pokes at the water.

"We need to tell people about this! They could test it! If it's clean here, that means it's probably clean in other places, too! This could change everything!"

"You're right, it would change everything. It would make the government powerless and create chaos all over again. People would think they could survive without the government just like before. And people would panic. I don't know about you, but I've heard the stories. People thinking they're safe on their own, and they no longer need the government. People tried to clean their own water once before, and the effects were catastrophic. Crowds of people dead in the streets. I'm not sure there would be a second recovery."

I look at him, slightly jealous of his unshakable confidence in the country's leadership. He has no idea I was one of those people who thought I could survive on my own. He has no idea that being trapped inside those gates is nothing but the worst of it. Outside this rubble lay masses of green. It may be far. But nevertheless, it's there. I may not have gotten far enough to see it, but I still know. "I think people deserve more trust than that. We learned our lesson. All they have to do is give us a chance."

"Maybe. Maybe not. Time will tell, and until then, I'll keep my thirst contained to water I don't need to worry about."

"Is that why you brought us here? To prove to me, I don't know what I'm doing? Because trust me, Kye. I already know that." My eyes watch Austin poke and prod the murky water. "I've known that my whole life."

I move away from the water and sit down next to Kye with my hands on the dirt behind me. How long will it be before the grass starts growing again?

"I'm not saying the government is right in everything they do, but they are right about the water. They know what they're doing." He gazes at the horizon, the water in front of us, and the little boy happily enjoying his new adventure. "But what I did to you was wrong. Josh was right. I should have either turned down the assignment or walked away from you. I may not have known who you were when I first saw you, but I should have acted differently once I did. I could be fired, fined, moved to another town, imprisoned, or, God forbid, something worse. It shouldn't have happened, and I'm sorry."

I look away, not wanting him to see the hurt in my eyes. But I'm also angry he changed the subject so quickly. He took something I cared so deeply about, like my hatred for the government, and turned it into an apology speech. "Then tell me why it did."

"Because I look at you and my job no longer matters. My assignment doesn't matter, Josh doesn't matter, and nothing else I have ever known matters. You're different from anyone I have ever known, and I can't get my mind off you. I've tried. God, I've tried so damn hard… but then I look at you and see all the pain you hold in your eyes. You try so hard to hide it."

"Don't you dare tell me you want to fix me. Don't you dare coddle me or treat me like a wounded puppy."

"No, no you're misunderstanding. I commend you. You go day to day, holding your head high. You keep it in as if you're trying to prove to the world that you don't need sympathy and that you're stronger than what people see. I'm trying to tell you that when people look at you, all they see is strength. I look in those eyes, and I wish I could learn your secrets. I wish I had that strength for myself." He bows his head. "I wish I were lucky enough for you to let me in." He looks sideways at me. "But what I did was wrong and a definite conflict with my job. And maybe still, maybe I'm not sorry."

I turn to look at him, staring at me.

"Here's the thing, Sara. I'm keeping my job, and I plan to keep my intentions toward you. I know I'm going to make a mess of things no matter what I do, but that's where it is. I'm not willing to give up you or my job. I'm damned if I do, but damned if I don't."

We sit in silence for a few minutes. I look away, not quite knowing what to say. Austin has scared away the fish and is throwing everything he can find into the water. Splashing stones and rippled currents keep him thoroughly entertained. I search the water for some sign of life but find it futile.

"So what now?"

He moves to stand up as I ask the question. Reaching down, he helps me up. "That's up to you. Ask me to kiss you again, and I'll never stop. Ask me never to touch you again, and it will break my heart. But I promise you; I'll honor your request."

Brushing the dirt off my pants, I look around nervously. I bite my nails. I don't know what to say, and I don't know what to do. Before I am allowed a chance to think, he has held me up and has his lips against mine. My heart stops, and I'm kissing him back.

I pull away and turn my back to him. I don't have the courage, though, and my lip quivers as he pulls me back to him. Taking a deep breath and biting my lower lip, I try to compose myself.

"I meant, what do we do about Austin," I say.

He looks at Austin and shakes his head, obviously dismissing my attempts to stay upbeat. The sharpness of his blue eyes digs into my heart.

"You need to tell me how to get to your outside contact."

His tone is genuine, and in that instant, I know he has more conflict in his heart than he lets on. But I've messed up before, and I have never been good at recovering from mishaps. It's more than just my life at stake here.

"No."

"It's his only chance, Sara." His hands dig into his pockets. "I know I say a lot of things. I know it's crystal clear to you that I trust our government and know their intentions are pure. But I also know you're right when you talk about what would happen to him if he is turned over to the detention center. You can't keep him safe anymore. Your contact is his only chance."

"And what happens to me once I give you his name? You take

me for all I am worth and shut the whole thing down?" My eyes glare into his. "You hang me out to dry, and that's the end of me?"

"I'd like to think you trust me a bit more than that."

"Well, I don't."

"Then I will stay here and wait. However long it takes for you to get Austin somewhere safe, with someone on the outside where he has a better chance."

I'm not sure what it is about Kye, but something inside him is screaming to be a good person. It's like he has it all backwards. He thinks his motivations are wrong and what the world has already set in place is good.

"Sooner or later, they will euthanize him, Sara."

"Then why do you keep working for them? Standing by when you know how terrible they make it for us?"

"After meeting Austin, I'm not quite sure anymore."

He walks closer to the water's edge and bends down to meet Austin eye to eye. Pulling him in for an embrace, Austin drops the rock he is holding firm in his grip and wraps his arms around Kye's neck. "I have to say goodbye now, buddy, okay? Sara will take you somewhere safe, and I'll wait right here for her to come back. But I'm not going to see you again, okay." His eyes are filled with moisture as he pushes Austin away and looks him in the face.

Austin stares at him expressionless but nods his head as though he understands.

Taking Austin out of Kye's grip, I walk him out of Kye's sight.

"What do you think the ocean is like? Do you think it's made of salt, as they say? Do you think it's clear as the water from our sinks?"

"I think you're obsessed. Why do you want to see the ocean so bad?" I say.

"I want to see what was here on Earth way before people ruined the ground with ugly buildings and concrete streets. Before the gray skies and the black

ground. I want to see what the Earth was supposed to look like. What it was meant to smell like."

"I think maybe it's because you want to be free. No laws, no codes, no people around telling you what to do all of the time. It's no longer just my dream, Tommy. It's yours now, too."

"Maybe. Maybe."

"I want you to be free too, Tommy. I want you to stop worrying so much about me. About everyone. Maybe at the ocean, you can let yourself just be."

"I will always worry about you, Princess. That's what it means to love someone. You make sure they are safe, and you make sure they are happy. It's impossible to be happy with so many stupid codes."

He jumps up and stretches his arms out to me. I smile and laugh as he begins to sing. Bending down, he grabs my hands and pulls me up to stand next to him. His arms wrap around my waist, and he twirls me. We spin and laugh; then stop twirling and dance to the music he hums. As we dance, I think maybe he is right. At the ocean, I wouldn't have anxiety about this moment ending. I wouldn't have to worry about making it to my chores on time or finding a job when I grow up. This moment could last forever.

"I'll be happy anywhere with you, Tommy." I feel like the music in my head will last forever.

Chapter 18

Dishwashers and washing machines are not allowed for private use. Water rations will incur when services are provided for citizens.

It's dark by the time I reach Maddox, and I can't help but be surprised and pleased I found my way at all. I figured I would not make it between the dusk and my original starting point. But I found my way back to the main road, then trekked the four miles northwest. Tommy once told me the easiest way to track directions was to follow the sun with your eyes. To imagine where it came from and predict where it is going next. The day the sun stops rising in the east, he said, was the day our time had come.

My arms ache from carrying Austin and my heart pounds. All I can think about is whether Maddox can give Austin a home and a better chance at life. Or just another place to wait for the next meal?

Maddox does not live in a house. It is not an apartment or even a crumpled down shack. He lives in a cellar with two hefty steel doors and a handful of ventilation shafts. Most of the doors cannot be seen from the outside. They are covered with the neglected and cracking concrete from the nearby gas station. Unless a person knew he was there, he would never be found.

I bang my fist on the steel doors. After only a few short moments, he cracks the door open and smirks as he sees me.

"Sara!" He embraces me in a hug. "What are you doing out here?"

"I need your help, Maddox." I shift Austin onto my opposite hip. "I'm sorry I came without any warning."

"No apologies necessary. Come on inside."

He holds open his door, ushers us inside, and double locks the door behind us. He sits me down on the sofa. I shift Austin to a sitting position on my lap. He rubs his groggy eyes.

"I heard what happened to Tommy. I am so sorry, Sara."

It's funny how information travels, even when word of mouth is separated by a ten-foot steel gate.

My thoughts get jumbled, and I ignore his apology about something he had no control over. The last thing I need right now is more emotions. I can barely handle the torment over Austin that already stacks up in my thoughts. Any more mention of Tommy and his death, and I may lose it completely.

Maddox pushes his dark, tangled hair out of his face as he listens to my story, as I plead for him to take Austin and deliver him someplace safe.

"Why don't you take him yourself?" he says.

"I don't have as many contacts as you do. Or the resources." A tear drops from my face. "I couldn't even help keep Tommy alive. What good could I possibly do for a three-year-old child? I need him with someone I can trust."

"You got him this far, didn't you?" he says.

I rub my hand through Austin's hair. "A few miles is very different than what I am asking of you."

"No kidding," he says. He stands up and paces in front of the door. "I could take him south, but I've never done it with a kid before. I have no idea how long it would take. Do you think he would be up for the journey?"

"He has to be." Another tear falls down my cheek. Austin's hands fold over mine. So petite. So tiny. Yet so filled with life.

I glance around the tiny room. Candlelight dances with Maddox's movements. And then he stops, and the flames seem to stand still. His eyes furrow in deep thought.

"Why won't you come with us?" he says.

The tears no longer stream down my face one by one. They flow in unison, and even as I close my eyes to stop them, they flow nevertheless. My breath quickens, and I squeeze my arms around Austin. He leans his head back to rest on my shoulder and softly pats my hands.

"I don't know." I shake my head in dismay. "I just can't."

Maddox plops down on the sofa next to us and wraps his arm around me. "I'm not sure when I will be back. If I will be back," he says.

"I'll keep up with ration drops anyway. Just in case." I understand how much of a burden I am asking him to take on. But I don't have any other options.

He nods his head. "At least stay with him for a few days while I pack up and get us ready. I know it's cramped, but I'll make room for you."

"I can't, Maddox. There's too much at stake." I run my fingers through Austin's hair one last time. "Be good little guy, okay?"

I stand up and turn his body, so we are in a full embrace. I let go of the breath I did not realize I was holding. More tears drop onto Austin's face. He is snuggling against me, squeezing so tight, I know he understands. He knows exactly what is happening here. It isn't even the first time this month he has been abandoned.

Maddox did not promise me anything, but he could find Austin a better life than I could imagine. Even as he hugs me goodbye, the pressure of his grip gives me hope.

I wait to fall apart until after he closes the door behind me, and I stumble my way through the darkness. Then I fall to the dirt-encrusted ground and will myself the energy to keep moving. I cry for Austin, and I cry for me. I cry because I could not get the words out of my mouth to tell him goodbye. And all the while, I keep telling myself over and over that it is okay. This is for the better.

I did not have to turn back and go home. I could have stayed with Austin, and I could go wherever Maddox had planned for him. We could go together. Yet I keep on walking. I walk over the dirt and dusty trail with the sun no longer guiding my path. I walk until my tears are dry, my heart is numb, and my feet blistered. I could barely do Austin right on the inside. How could I possibly do any better on the outside? Dr. Hammid's voice rings imaginary lectures in my mind. *If I cannot take care of myself, how can I possibly care for someone else?*

I reach Kye in the morning. His body is slumped next to a tree trunk long since perished. But he stirs the moment he hears my feet rustling through the foliage, and he lets me fall into him. I rest my head on his shoulder without any words about how it went. And bless his heart, he never once asks. I cry so hard his shirt must be soaking wet, and never once does he complain. I am not sure how long we sit together, but my stomach is growling, and my mouth is parched by the time I stand.

"Time to go?" he says.

I nod, once again analyzing his character, how he justified what we just did, his part in helping Austin to get away, and my decision to come back. I wonder if he worried about my return.

We are walking back to the Jeep when he asks about the bookstore in an attempt to get our minds off Austin, off his choices, and even some of mine.

"It was kind of a dream I fell into. Reading has always been my escape, so it makes sense that I do what I can to spread the passion. The store was a good way to keep up my inheritance. Josh is working hard to put all the legalities into my name." I feel guilty bringing him up, and that guilt descends into regret.

Kye pushes fallen tree branches out of our path. "Sara, I know Josh left, and I want you to know I think it's good for you. I think it is for the better."

I feel myself reflexively getting defensive over Josh. "I think it's best if you leave it alone. It's not your family that you keep talking trash about."

"He isn't safe to be around, and I'm not sure why you don't understand that. We have a file on him a mile deep, and I can't figure out how you fit into the picture for the life of me. Why the hell are you so defensive about him?"

"How can you be so misinformed?"

"By all means then, Sara, inform me."

It takes me a while; soon, the words pour out of me.

"I met Josh when I was six. My family had just moved into town after the water was cut off. His mom sent him and his little brother out on a scavenging run. Tommy saw me unpacking and asked if I would tag along. I did, of course, and Tommy introduced me to dirt boarding. We were three miles from home, and I surfed down a dirt hill on a rusted-out shutter. Needless to say, I didn't do so well, and Josh carried me all the way home. Tommy came over every single day for months, waiting for my ankle to heal. He said he had never known a girl like me, and when I was all healed up, I had to teach him how to fly like that. We became inseparable. He had that effect on people. Had the same effect on Josh, anyway. He had my back as he did Tommy's.

"But Tommy and I had different ideas about the world than Josh. Josh went with the flow. Whereas Tommy always argued the flow's direction. We were barely fifteen when we decided to leave. We wanted Josh to come with us and spent weeks begging him, but he refused. Said there are better ways to fix the world than walk away from the cause of the problems. But that's the thing about Josh. He always does the unexpected. Without a goodbye or any kind of warning, he left for Zone Four. At the time, I didn't even know.

"Tommy and I left, too. We made it to the edge of the desert, where we came across a group of people camped by a fire. We were so close to the ocean we could almost smell it. The air was actually wet. I felt it in my chest when I breathed."

The snap of the twigs under my feet grow harder to focus on as the memories flood me. "They offered us food and a place to stay the night." I hear the panic in my voice as I quiver. "I fell asleep before dinner was cooked. Tommy woke me up twice. Once to offer me dinner, and once more to move me into an abandoned cabin. The next morning, I woke up to Tommy burning with fever and our campmates dead beside the burned-out fire." I pause. "I did everything I could. He died within two days."

"How did he die?" Kye said.

"Just like everyone else on the outside. Dirty water poisoned him." I pause in my story and try to regain my composure. "Scavengers found me dehydrated and clinging to his lifeless body.

They took me to the first patrol stand they found. They thought that in my condition, they were the only chance I had. After weeks in a cleanup camp, enforcements finally swept through, and I was transported back here. My DNA swab had been flagged."

"Why?"

"Frank had been looking for us. He sent out massive search parties to find us. Because I left of my own free will, I was never supposed to be allowed back through the gates, but Frank testified in front of a jury that Tommy had brainwashed me. That none of it was my idea. Josh was so pissed when he found out. He was infuriated that his father would turn his back on his own dead son, and even in death refuse to admit that he had neglected to love him for the person he was."

I climb over fallen branches. "I haven't spoken to Frank since. Josh showed up shortly after that. He ranted and raved about how it was his fault and how sorry he was for abandoning not only Tommy but also me. He's been there for me ever since."

Kye slides into the driver's seat of the Jeep and sits there with the engine off. Looking at me. As if he finally understands, he leans in and grabs my hands from my knees. "Sara, I'm so sorry."

"He is the only family I have left. I know you have a job to do, and you think something is going on that isn't, but I'm telling you, I'm asking you to leave my family alone."

He just sits next to me as I let the memories of my past live themselves out all over again. Several minutes go by before I break the silence. "Kye, I want to know why. I mean since I was a kid all I've known is Enforcements arresting and charging people with crimes and breaking codes well before they have proof of injustice. Why is Josh being treated differently? If everyone thinks he is so guilty, why hasn't he been hanged?"

"We were told not to touch him. Warned that the situation needed cleanup and permission from command before he is ever touched or arrested. That permission only comes with proof that he killed Janson Thomas."

"From command or from Frank Lorenzo? That sounds like more of a red flag than anything else. I'm shocked you didn't question that."

"We did. Niles is still on it every damn day. But Command is command. There is nothing we can do."

Kye finally starts the Jeep, and we ride home in silence. He continues to hold my hand as we bump and dip over rubble. We are let through the gates with no questions asked. All it takes is a display of Kye's badge. He pulls into my drive as the sun begins to set. I feel empty without Austin at my side. More alone than ever.

"If you two are as close as you say you are, ask him. Ask him what he got involved with over that period of two years and why his mentor is dead. Ask him why the government patrols are watching his every move and why the hell he hasn't warned you about any of it. Ask him how he can look you in the face and pretend his friendship with you doesn't put you in danger. Better yet, the next time you see him, ask him how he can abandon his so-called family over and over again."

"Meredith, have you seen my blue striped button-down shirt?"

We all sit at the table eating cereal as Frank walks into the kitchen.

"Yeah, it's dirty. Bottom of the hamper in the bedroom."

"I need you to have it picked up for wash tomorrow."

"Sorry. But no, it can't be done." She bites her lip, nervous about how he will respond.

We all drop our spoons and look up at her. No one says no to Frank. Ever.

"I'm sorry? No? Why the hell not?"

"We don't have enough water rations. I can't send out any more laundry

until this water cycle is up."

She turns to clear the cereal boxes off the table, never looking at any of us.

"Hand wash it, then. I don't care how, just get it done."

"I'm telling you that it can't be done. We don't have enough water left in this cycle."

"We have five days left in THIS cycle. What the hell happened?"

She does not respond. She just continues to clean up the morning mess.

"MEREDITH! What the hell happened?"

"I don't know. I haven't been thinking clearly, I guess. I've been drinking more water than my fair share."

She sits down at the table next to Tommy and brushes his hair out of his face with her dainty fingers.

"You DRANK it? There are five people in this house. How could you possibly drink so much water?"

He storms over to the table, bends down, and glares at her—inches from her face.

Tommy stands up. "She's pregnant, dad. She's been showing for weeks. We'll get through the next five days. It's no big deal."

"Pregnant? Are you freaking kidding me? Did everyone know about this except for me?" He steps closer to Tommy, asking everyone the question yet directing it to Tommy only.

"You're an idiot," Tommy says.

He takes a step closer to his father.

Frank turns back to Meredith, sitting at the table and slaps her across the face. "I need that shirt by tomorrow. Figure it out."

He turns and walks out of the house.

Meredith stands up and starts cleaning the kitchen.

Tommy takes the silverware out of her hands. "Go lay down, mom. We'll take care of it. We'll take care of all of it."

She kisses him on the cheek and leaves the kitchen.

Chapter 19

The remains of the deceased will be handed over to government officials for proper disposal.

I don't stick around to argue. Getting out of the car, I slam the door. I gaze down the street. Dead trees line the long curving driveway, making it difficult to see. Before the government transformation, cars would have screeched up and down the street, their headlights lighting up the driveway. Now, all I hear is silence through the darkness. I push my way into the house and leave Kye alone with his misguided thinking.

I head into the kitchen and pull down the bottle of wine hidden over the fridge. I force my shaking body onto a barstool and drink straight from the bottle. I'm positioned to look directly at Josh's closed bedroom door. He did not get a chance to say goodbye to Austin.

Josh has issues. I know that. I've always known that, but I have never once thought of him as abandoning me on purpose. He does his own thing, but he always comes back. He has always come back. I keep drinking and thinking about how he walks away. Time and time again. Every time things get a little rough, he walks away. The bottle is empty before I realize how much I drank.

I throw the bottle of wine at his bedroom door in an angered attempt to stop thinking about him. The truth hits me like a crashing meteor. Maybe Kye is right. Every one of Josh's actions has been based on selfish desires.

I'm pretty drunk by the time the second bottle feels light in my hands. I crawl towards his door, away from the safety of my bar stool. I see nothing but emptiness behind it. I place my palm on the wood. How did everything get so messed up? Hanging my head, I cry. All I ever do now is cry.

When all my tears have fallen, and I feel like I have nothing else to give, I pull myself up and stumble to my room on the other side of the house. Trying to place the bottle of wine on my nightstand, I stumble and knock my pills all over the floor. The left-over wine gurgles as it pours out of the bottle and makes a giant red stain on the carpet. Sliding down next to the mess, I lean my back against the bed for support. I close my eyes and force my mind to turn off.

"Tommy! Josh! Tommy! Josh!"

I'm screaming their names as loud as I can as I run back to the house. My chest hurts from running so far, but I fear I'm not running fast enough. "Tommy! Josh!"

The screen door slams shut as both boys rush out of the house.

"What? What's the matter?"

"Meredith. She's … she's…" I'm gasping for breath. "She's in the reservoir." I bend my knees and grab them for support.

"In the reservoir?" Their question comes out in unison.

"She climbed the fence. She's SWIMMING in the reservoir."

Before I can finish catching my breath, both of them rush past me. I race back to where I was when it all started.

When we reach the reservoir at the edge of town, the giant steel fence surrounding the complex stops us. But we can clearly see Meredith. She is on her back, with her bare feet kicking in the water underneath her. Her arms reach behind her head one at a time as she glides around the giant pool. She is wearing Frank's blue-striped, button-down shirt.

"Mom! Mom! What are you doing! Get out! You need to get out!"

The screams echo across the land just as whistles begin to blow and seven armed enforcement cops reach the water's edge. All with guns pointed at her head.

The tallest man in the officer's uniform screams at her. "Ma'am, you need to get out of the water! You need to get out of the water now!"

She stops swimming and bobs up and down in the water. Her long brunette hair lays on the soft current like a sheet. Perfect as always. Her wet clothes stick to her like melting wax on a candle. She twists her body and opens her eyes to look at the three of us plastered up against the nine-foot fence. A soft smile creeps onto her face, though sadness fills her eyes. We can't hear her, but her words are unmistakable. "I love you all."

Her body sinks, and the beautiful woman who helped raise me, cared for me when my own mother couldn't, who loved me, who sang to me night after night, disappears beneath the water. The screams next to me are so loud that I can't be certain they aren't my own. The fence in front of me is shaking. Both boys are climbing the fence in front of me, racing to the top.

The guards argue about not knowing how to swim. One screams about contaminating the water. Another is shooting random shots into the water. Tommy and Josh both cross the top of the fence and dive headfirst into the sparkling clear water. I stand alone, crying at the fence as a crowd gathers behind me.

I don't think to count how many more shots are fired. I don't think about the splashing water or the change in the current around Meredith. I don't think about the silence that follows. All I can think about is how quickly the *watercolor changes. Red spills everywhere. It feels like minutes pass, with all three of them underwater. Then I see three heads bob to the surface. I can't tell if she is still breathing. I can barely tell if I'm breathing.*

All three of them are pulled from the water. Tommy and Josh are arrested and put into a detention center for three months. We never see Meredith again. She receives no gravestone.

Chapter 20

No female shall birth more than two children.

I wake up to my cheeks in Josh's hands. He is shaking me, begging me to wake up. I think it's real, but I can't be sure this is not a dream. I am still on the floor, sitting in a puddle of wine.

Kneeling in front of me, with his face inches from my own, he is talking to me in a panicked tone. But the alcohol in my system won't let me concentrate on the words coming out of his mouth, and my eyes hurt to open as his voice gets louder and louder.

"How many did you take?"

The squeeze of his fingers on my chin hurts as he pulls my head up to his own.

"W-What? W-What are you doing? C-Can't do this with you now. I need to sleep." I'm struggling to stay awake as he holds up my head, both hands now on my cheeks.

"How many did you take?"

He's pulling at my eyes, using my arm to help keep me steady. I hear the concern in his voice but can't understand the cause of his urgency and concern.

"Sara, I'm not messing around. How many pills did you take?"

My eyes flutter to the pills spilled on the floor next to me. "None. I don't. I didn't. None."

I try to stand up, but I stumble, and I can't hold up my own weight.

"Are you lying to me?"

His hand is still holding my chin inches from his face as I try and pull away. "No. You're the only one who does all the lying."

"I deserve that and probably much worse."

He stands and pulls my limp body up to the bed. After forcing my wine-stained pants off, he pulls the covers over me. My eyes close as I sense his hesitation.

The pressure of the mattress shifts, and he lays down next to me. "Promise me you didn't take any?"

I don't have enough energy to answer him. I feel his fingers trying to find the pulse on my neck. I know he finds it, but a part of me can only imagine what he thinks of me right now. What he thinks I did. Maybe neither of us knows the other as we thought.

We are all silent at the table. Eating rations that taste like cardboard. Josh and Tommy both came home from detention looking thinner. Loss remains apparent on both of their sad faces.

It's Frank who finally breaks the silence. "Some exciting news with the government is about to transpire. I recently passed a bill making it illegal for couples to have more than two children."

We drop our utensils and stare at him.

He continues to eat with a smug look on his face, as if he is proud of himself. "What? No congratulations?"

We continue to stare without saying a word.

"Three is too much. I learned that the hard way. People will be better off with only two. Trust me. This is a good thing."

Tommy stands up and pushes his chair back first, glaring at his father. Instinctively, Josh and I move back from the table as Tommy flips the entire table towards Frank. Food and utensils fly into the air, clattering as they hit the ground.

Frank brushes the food off his lap and calmly approaches Tommy. Tommy has nowhere to go but back against the wall. Frank's right-hand clasps Tommy's neck while his left-hand braces himself against the wall. He pulls Tommy's feet off the floor in the process.

"Accept your place in the world, boy, and get over yourself."

He throws Tommy to the floor just as Josh jumps over the broken table. "Let Tommy go!"

Frank drops Tommy and walks out of the kitchen laughing. All we can do is watch, knowing with dark certainty that Frank was responsible for Meredith's death.

Chapter 21

Aerators and/or water flow attachments must be used in all residences and public places of business. Any misuse of water must be reported to Water Systems Inc.

I wake up to find Josh still lying on the bed next to me, about a foot from my face. I don't know what to think about him being here or why he felt the need to babysit me overnight. I'm not sure how long I slept, but the aching behind my eyes is yearning for painkillers.

I crawl out of bed and head for the kitchen. The clock reads past noon as I shuffle in. I should be at the store today, but that's obviously not going to happen. Or maybe it was a shrink day. I don't even know. After I wash up, I pour myself some coffee.

Josh stands in the doorway staring at me. "How are you feeling?"

"Fine." I feel like my insides have been torn out. "Where have you been?"

He responds with a question of his own. "What happened here last night?"

"Nothing."

"Obviously. Where is Austin, Sara?"

"I got him out. They found out I had him, and there were no papers and no way to keep him, so I got him out."

His silence penetrates the room, eating at my flesh like pins and needles. Is his silence a sign of approval or dismay? My head hurts so much I can't determine the difference. But thinking of Austin, thinking of him on the outside, not even sure if he has eaten today, makes me crumble to the floor all over again.

"I don't know what to say. You scared the hell out of me last night. Talk to me. What happened?"

"Nothing happened. You were gone, just like always. Austin was gone, too. And it was all because of me—all of it. So I drank. I cried, and then I drank some more. End of story." My fingers grip the side of the coffee cup as I wait for the tension to cool. "What I would like to know is where you have been."

"I was helping Rick with a few things at work."

He moves closer to me. He has bags under his eyes, his face is unshaven, and he carries an invisible weight on his shoulders. He slides down to the floor next to me.

"How coincidental."

"Sara, I think it's time we talk."

I don't respond, but I look up, squishing my lips. He should have talked to me months ago. Maybe even years. "I'm listening."

I force myself to stand and stroll over to the living room. I pour myself onto the sofa and pretend not to care as I sip my coffee. Maybe weak-ass caffeine will take away my headache.

He sits next to me, takes a deep breath, and begins to talk to me like Tommy used to.

"I knew dad looked for you two after you split. I don't think he ever really understood that I knew. I also knew that he was looking for you out of pride. He was a typical politician more concerned about saving face than what was going on with his own son. I was so angry that he blamed Tommy for the whole thing. I was mad that I had let you two leave. Even more furious that I left without letting you guys know. At first, I drank away my anger. Then I met Janson. I must have been ranting and raving one night about how I blamed myself and how I should have figured out a way to make you stay. I should have figured out a way to save mom. There are so many things I should have done.

"After sobering me up, Janson took me to Water Systems. I was furious. Told him that he had missed the entire point of my anger and that the water was the cause of it all." He pauses in his story yet continues to stare at the floor. "He showed me a few things. Some pretty impressive things, and I was intrigued. He taught me how it was done and got me a job I gladly accepted."

Once more, he pauses in his story. This time he glances up at me as if gauging my reaction. I'm not as relaxed on the couch as I was minutes prior, but I am sure that the look of confusion on my face is unmistakable.

"Sara, he taught me how to steal water and pump it into people's homes without anyone ever knowing. With just a few codes in a computer, it's undetectable. Anyone looking at the paperwork still sees rations set in stone per water laws."

"How do they not know? How is there enough in the reservoirs?"

"There is no shortage of water. That's a myth. A myth that anyone without clearance would be killed for if it got out."

"Where do you pump it? Who gets the water you take?"

"Anyone with kids under two. Anyone over seventy. Plus a few others, of course. I would give it to everyone if I could, but it's hard enough getting in and out of the system unnoticed. When I got transferred back here, I started pumping water to Zone One and a little to Two and Three. Janson maintained control over Zone Four."

"Why haven't any of these people come forward and informed code enforcement that they were getting extra water?"

"They don't know. The meter reads what it should. But the meters are pre-set. They will never run out of water in those homes."

"What do you mean they don't know? How could they not know?"

Finally, turning his head to look at me, his hands fold into his lap. "Did you know?"

I'm speechless as I try and put it all together. Minutes pass as we stay seated there, with me pondering it over and over. I finally find the words I know Josh won't be happy to hear. "Josh, what you're doing, it's meaningless unless they know. You're not God. You can't hope that people will take advantage of what you're doing for them. When Robin Hood stole money for the poor, the poor knew."

"If they don't run out of water, they won't leave. If they don't run out of water, they don't intentionally drown themselves. I know that your opinion is different than mine. It always has been. But I'm trying to keep these people alive. As many as I can. Even if they don't know it."

"And everyone else? What about them?"

"I can only do so much," he whispers, regret in his voice.

I can't help but stand up and pace the floor in front of him. "What happened to Janson?"

"A pipe blew in Benford in Zone Four. Instead of turning off the damn pipe, they thought they would wait for the water to run out. Wait till the resident rations ran out, and the pipe would dry out. But it never did. The town flooded. People were outraged. They honestly thought the government was wasting their water and condemning them to death. Officials went to Janson because he had control over that line. He was dead the next day."

I stop pacing and stare at him.

"I was called in to try and clean up the mess, but with so many eyes on Benford, I couldn't do a whole lot. If I fixed the rations the way they wanted, they would know I was in on it all along. I sent Rick up there to maintain what had already been started."

"Josh, if they knew, you would be done for. Just like Janson."

He moves to the mantel and stares at the photo of Tommy. "I know. I've tried to cut things back slowly, but with so many eyes on me, I can't just shut down the system. I need to remain inconspicuous. Reducing rations would cause more eyes to look in my direction."

"Are you saying our government had Janson killed? To save face?"

"I don't know who did it. I just know that because I was seen leaving Janson's house hours before he was found dead, I'm the one enforcement is looking at. He called me in a panic. I showed up and searched through his files, making sure there was no trail. But it all led straight to him. He should have run. That was my only advice after trying so hard to prevent people like Tommy from leaving. But Janson was just as strong-willed as Tommy, and he ignored me anyway."

I sit on the sofa. My head is spinning, and my nausea is increasing. "Does Niles suspect you with the water? Or does he think you were the one who killed Janson?"

"I don't know. I was kind of hoping you would."

"Kye is clueless about the water. But I think he and Niles have always been on two different pages."

I feel like my world is spinning. Like everything I have ever known is about to be pulled from under me. "What if you went public with it? If people knew there is enough water, it wouldn't matter. People would overthrow the government in a heartbeat."

"I've thought about that. I still think they would kill me. I think I need to let things be. Keep going as I have been. Keep those people hydrated at all costs. That was my original intention. I don't think it should change."

His voice lays soft on my thoughts.

"You're missing the main problem. Stop thinking about all those people who take you for granted. Worry about yourself for once. What happens if one of *your* lines breaks? What happens to you then?"

His face is flat, and the answer is written all over it. He slowly sinks into the cushions on the couch. "I've pulled the numbers. I don't think the system was built to hold the pressure Janson and I have been pumping through it. His numbers were higher than mine, but I'm not far behind. I don't think it's *if;* I think it's *when.* But Sara, someone has some pull out there. Someone is keeping me alive." He runs his fingers through his hair. "Otherwise, Enforcement would have had me hanged long ago. I think you know that."

He refuses to look at me. He knows what I am going to say. "No. Absolutely not okay. Dammit, Josh! You're all I have freaking left!" I feel my cheeks burn red as I scream at him.

He turns to me, his eyes haunted. "First of all, calm down. Second of all, it's been fine for years. I'm sure it will be fine for many, many more."

"But you don't know. Every option you have ends with you being killed. Or some unknown guardian keeping you from being killed. I'm not losing you. I'm not losing another Lorenzo."

He stands up and walks over to me at the mantel. "What do you want to do, Sara? Tell me what to do."

"I don't know. I don't know. I don't know." The silence permeates the room as I struggle to maintain my composure. "The beach," I whisper. "Let's go to the beach. It's what Tommy would have told you to do. It's what you told Janson to do. Let's leave." My words come out barely audible, knowing full well what he will say.

"No. No way in hell. It didn't work out last time for you. I do what I do to prevent people from leaving. I do it to keep you healthy and alive. There is no way."

We slide down the wall next to the fireplace. Folding my knees into my chest, I rest my head on his shoulder. He wraps his arm around me.

"Last time was different. And if it works for Austin, there is no reason it can't work for us."

Last time I did not plan ahead enough. Last time I did not know what to expect. "Do you remember that pond west of the east entrance? Before the gates were put up? We used to go there as kids and watch the water levels drop." I feel the tears forming in my eyes. "We always wanted to see who could get close enough to the water and breathe in the stench the longest."

"Yeah, Tommy always won." He smirks and snort-laughs. "It was always so rancid."

"I was there yesterday. A fish is in the pond, Josh. A real fish with an orange tail and a head almost silver like the sun. If the fish are back, that means the water has healed. It will be safer this time. We could make it. Just like Austin."

I know he hears the hope in my voice. Oh God, how I wish I could make it to the beach.

"You're telling me you saw a fish?"

"Yes, yes I am. It was as beautiful as a rainbow."

"How do you know someone didn't just put it there?"

"I don't. But it means hope for us, Josh. Please. Please, let's just go."

"No. I can't do it. I can't let something bad happen to you again. It's not worth it, Sara. It's not."

"So, what happens to me if we stay? Your pipe breaks, or you get caught? Either way, you're saying you're dead, or your so-called guardian changes his mind. What happens to me then?"

He doesn't answer right away. He knows I'm right. If what he said to me the other day was true, then he can't let it happen. He just can't.

"Give me another option," he says.

I pull my head off his shoulder. Last night I was furious at him for always leaving. Now, it's the only thing I want from him. "Quit your job. Walk away."

He laughs and pulls his arms away. "Your ideas are terrible. If I don't have a job, I lose my food rations. You know this."

"How can you possibly laugh at a time like this?"

He doesn't answer me; he just smirks as he looks at me. Minutes pass, and I have nothing for him. No ideas. No piece of hope aside from finally getting to the ocean. "Talk to Frank. Maybe he can get you transferred. Maybe in another zone away from here just in case anything ever happened with those pipes."

"Not without you. And even if I got dad on my side with the Senate's vote, they would never allow it."

"Then you go without me."

"You want me to leave?"

"No, I want you to live. Of course, I don't want you to leave. I'm so tired of you leaving. But … I need you around. I want you around. Even if it's just occasionally."

He doesn't respond, just stares at me with a blank expression. I know it's a stupid idea, but it's all I have. "Maybe I can sell the idea to Dr. Hammid. I need to move my store to another zone to help me move away from the gravestones I use as anchors or the childhood memories that won't let me sleep."

"I can tell you right now; it won't work. You're lucky that your shop hasn't rendered you into a starving frenzy, but let me think about it, okay? Let me feel out my boss. Dad maybe. I'd need to sell him on the idea of going with you." He pulls me closer. "But Sara, even moving to another zone, it's a band-aid. You know, that, right?"

I wrap my arms around him and let the tears fall.

"Josh, come with us."

"No. I'm sorry, but no. It's not the way to save things. There has to be another way. I have to believe there's another way."

"I can't stay here, Josh. I can't live like this. This isn't what life was supposed to be about. I hate it. I hate eating what they tell me. I hate that I can only go outside when they tell me it's okay. I hate that I have to clean up their mess, and yet they never attempt to make things better for us. I want to be free of them. I want to be free of HIM!"

"I get it, Tommy. Trust me; I get it. And I will do everything I can for you two. But I can't go with you. I have a pull here. I need to make sure he doesn't get any more codes passed. But think this through. You have no idea how to survive out there."

Josh shakes his head at Tommy and walks out of the room.

We don't see Josh for dinner that night. We don't see him as we pack. And turning back to look at the house in the dark of the night, we don't see him as we leave.

Chapter 22

All citizens must remain inside government-proclaimed

safety zones.

Josh leaves for the train the following day. Leaving me alone. I try to control my thoughts by moving through my typical morning routine. Any hope I had of a normal day comes to a halt when I hear the knock at the door. Two uniformed enforcement cops stand in front of me.

"Ms. Carson, you have missed three consecutive blood drops. We are required by the laws of all Clean Zones and the Citizens Government to take you in."

I'm an idiot. How the hell could I forget three drops in a row? "Can't I just give you a drop and be done with it?"

"Sorry, ma'am. You need to come cooperatively, or we will be forced to sedate you."

"Fine. Let me get my stuff."

"Sorry, ma'am. Shoes only. From this moment on, you may not

leave our side."

He gives me an annoyed look as if I am the one ruining *his* day. Yet all I can think is that Austin is safe from this man. Thank goodness Austin is gone.

They lead me to a black Jeep, identical to the one Kye had me riding in the other day. I can't help but wonder how they have so many matching cars since the world came crashing to a halt.

I'm led to the Code Office downtown. We pass a stone monument of a uniformed officer in front of the building. I walk up the twenty steps to the entrance. Filled with enforcement cops and lawbreakers, I wonder at the side I find myself on. Josh is stealing water from the government, and yet I am taken in for missing freaking blood drops.

They push me into a claustrophobic room with one table and two metal chairs. A window would be nice. Maybe even an offer to get me a cup of coffee.

I sit for what must be hours. The video camera hanging in the corner of the room follows my every move and taunts me like the thought of the coffee I still haven't been offered. Not that there is a whole lot of moving I can do. I walk around the table a few times. I even stand on the table in hopes of gaining some attention. But I am left to wait in silence, alone, for hours. Occasional footsteps walk past the door, but I have no idea how much time has passed. I know Kye is somewhere here. Are his footsteps the ones I hear pass by the door? My boredom actually makes my skin burn.

I am asleep in the metal chair with my face plastered against the matching metal table in front of me when the door finally opens. A medic comes in with a tiny handbag, not an inch of kindness anywhere on his face. He grabs my arm, takes my blood pressure, a swab from my mouth, and a vile of blood.

"I have to pee."

He stops what he is doing to look up from my arm.

A nod of his head is the only response I get. As soon as he completes his work, I am escorted to a small restroom outside my room. I gulp handfuls of water from the sink using my hands as cups. If I was to ask, they might even give me a glass.

Dr. Hammid is waiting in the gray room upon my return.

I don't even give her a chance to reprimand me. "Sorry, Doc. I don't know what happened."

I slump down in my chair as if I don't have a care in the world. But the truth is, I'm terrified, hungry as hell, and my ass hurts from sitting in this stupid chair all day.

"Sara, the conditions of your release into the Clean Zones were very clear. Breaking those conditions violates the law. Senator Lorenzo recommends that you be moved into the mental health detention center for permanent residency."

"WHAT?"

My knees are shaking as anger pulls me to my feet. "Are you kidding me?" I clench my hands into fists. My nails dig into my skin. "That dirty bastard! I swear to God, as soon as I am out of here …"

My words are cut off when Dr. Hammid places one index finger over her lips and shakes her head ever so slightly.

She is urging me to be quiet, warning me that I need to watch what I say. I take deep breaths. I sit down and try to get my pulse to slow. After several minutes, I glance at the security camera and lift my chin up. "I'm sorry. That reaction was uncalled for. Senator Lorenzo was like a father to me. A suggestion like that just surprised me. I apologize." I don't look back at the camera. I keep my eyes glued on Dr. Hammid, who may be more street-worthy than I initially gave her credit for.

A knock at the door interrupts our conversation. To my surprise, Kye walks in before a response is even offered. An officer comes in behind him carrying another small metal chair. He places it next to Dr. Hammid.

"Dr. Sylvia Hammid, it's nice to meet you." He places his hand out to greet her as she quickly stands to her feet. "My name is Kye. Kye Anslem. I hope you don't mind my presence here, but I believe I can offer you some assistance."

I squint at him. His presence here must mean I am in obvious need of a rescue. How often must he come back calmly after I storm away from him?

"How so, Mr. Anslem? We were just about to discuss sentencing."

His body is turned into her. She appears uneasy, even uncertain of herself. She pushes her frames higher on her nose and crosses her legs, pulling at the hem of her skirt, the long black stockings shimmering in the pale fluorescent lights.

His eyes never move off her, though. My presence is a ghost to both of them.

"You see, I have been dating Ms. Carson for a while now." He gestures at me with an embarrassed grin. "I was unaware of her code restrictions. As a matter of fact, I feel slightly responsible. I have been around a lot and feel like maybe I have been pushing her to do things that aren't in her typical routine. I'm worried that our new romance has gotten the best of her judgment and sense of responsibility."

A part of me hates him right now. Hates how his body is leaned into the doctor. Hates how he has made me seem like an incapable girl blinded by lust. Another part of me thinks he is brilliant.

"A romance?" Her eyes widen as she turns to look at me. "Sara! I had no idea. This is wonderful news!" She turns back to Kye and takes hold of his hands to cup them in her own. "Mr. Anslem, would you mind terribly giving me a few minutes? Let me see what I can do?"

"Of course. Take as much time as you need."

He squeezes her hands in his as she stands, a grin plastered all over her face.

Brilliant. Pure Brilliance.

As soon as the door closes, he turns to look at me. His smile is smug. "Sweetheart, what the hell were you thinking?" he whispers.

My use of the word is slightly more sarcastic than his. "Sweetheart, obviously, I wasn't." The look in his eyes is filled with care and concern. Utter bullshit. "How bad is it looking?"

"At the moment, it's pretty bad. I don't know what you did to piss off Senator Lorenzo, but he is livid. I honestly had no idea he was Josh's father. I thought the name was coincidental. I feel like such an idiot."

"Didn't I already tell you once that you weren't very good at your job?" I say.

He cocks his head. "But I am pretty good at a few other things.

Dr. Hammid returns with a grim look on her face. "I can do six months of house arrest, but that is the best I've got."

She returns to her seat and leans into Kye. "Mr. Anslem, you will escort Ms. Carson to and from weekly therapy sessions and personally see to it that medication is received and blood draws are taken and delivered routinely. Any breach will mean immediate removal from all Clean Zones."

She turns to me, a sad expression on her face. "I am so sorry, Sara."

She knows I will fail. It's only a matter of time.

Kye does not hesitate. "Agreed."

Both stand proudly and shake hands. Too bad their pride is

overshadowed by my bitterness.

"Have you ever seen anything so beautiful in your life?"

We walk hand in hand towards the mountains on the horizon. Orange and purples lie in the clouds that hang above the mountains. The tips converge with the clouds, and it takes me more focus than it should to decipher the difference between the sky and the snow-covered mountain tops. Watching such a scene unfold before me, I no longer think of the soreness of my feet or the rumbling in my belly.

I drop his hand and wrap my arm around the back of his waist as we walk.

Tommy looks ahead. "He would have liked it out here, you know. I don't care what he said. He would have liked it."

"I know. But I think that sometimes the world moves too fast for Josh. He needs to come to his own conclusions in his own time frame. But he'll figure it out one day. Sooner or later, he'll figure it out."

Chapter 23

No citizen may have a domestic or wild animal in their

care.

Kye walks me home, accepting the silence that is the only thing giving me comfort. Is it possible to get any darker in a world so filled with darkness?

The walk seems too short. I try to keep the pace slow, knowing it might be the last time I walk down these streets, but I am still forced to move forward step by step. I look towards the cemetery. When was the last time I went to see Tommy? How long will it be before I run my fingers across the carved rock?

Maybe I am being overly dramatic. Maybe six months isn't that bad. Maybe I can do it. Maybe I will surprise myself. Of course, it means I won't be able to eat out anymore. I will be stuck with tasteless government-engineered food rations three times a day. I won't be able to go to the thirst station. Not that I ever enjoyed it much in the first place. It also means Kye will be my babysitter for the next six months. I guess that will give him time to convince me of the romance we have going on, just as he did Dr. Hammid.

But what about Josh? What about my store? What about the notes I planned for Maddox, begging for some good news about Austin?

My mind wanders back to the fish as we walk up to my drive. A fish that represents hope. It would be different this time. I know how to prepare. I know how to survive. If I broke my house arrest intentionally, Josh would have no choice but to leave with me. He would not let me go alone. This punishment may actually be the push I need to get him to go with me. I could find Austin. But then again, what would happen to Kye?

Kye breaks the silence when we reach my front door. "I know you're not happy about this, Sara. But trust me when I tell you that it is the better option. Whoever goes in does not come out of the mental health facility. It's not the place for you."

I stop walking and contemplate his words.

"Why does he hate you so much? Senator Lorenzo, I mean. Why does he see you as such a threat to his community?" Kye says.

"It wasn't always like that. Over time it just got worse and worse. I guess I represent a part of his life he doesn't want to be reminded of anymore. His wife walked away. Both of his kids walked away. He tried keeping me around. Maybe for the memory of Meredith. Maybe because of Tommy. Maybe because he knew they would have wanted him to try. I don't really know. But in time, it changed, and now I'm a memory tied to all his failures. He tried to fix it. By then, it was too late. I guess instead of waiting for me to walk away, he is forcing my hand."

"That's ludicrous." His tone is flat.

Neither one of us moves to the door. Looking at him, I know he is contemplating my intentions and deciding whether I would do it or not. Walk away, that is.

"What time does Josh get home?

"How do you know he isn't home?" I say.

"It's my job."

I grinned. "But haven't I told you before that you aren't very good at your job?"

"I'm serious, Sara. What time does he get home?"

"Is that your plan? To place a babysitter on me full time? Make sure I won't run?" Maybe he is finally starting to understand me.

"If you need one, I will do what I need to do. You're fed here, Sara. You get food, water, and shelter whenever you need it. I am responsible for you, and it will be my ass if you run. Don't forget that."

"But maybe I need some sort of pet. Might be easier to have company if I'm stuck here by myself all day every day." I feel my eyes harden on him.

"You know that isn't going to happen." He says. "Thank you for the walk home. I'm going to lie down."

He steps in front of me and blocks my way to the door.

"Give it a chance. Give me a chance." His voice is stern.

I feel the water collect in my eyes. Kye isn't a bad guy. He is actually a really good one, but I have little hope here. I am way too flawed to be successful at house arrest. Doesn't he see that in me yet? Doesn't he see I am in the same position Austin was not so long ago?

"I have a lot to think about. But I guess I will see you in the morning, right? Since you are now my acting pill case?"

I take a deep breath and try to calm my out-of-control emotions. He needs to see me as strong and in control. He needs to see that making a decision like that will take some time. He continues to stare at me, with his eyes locked onto mine.

He nods his head slightly. "I'll be here bright and early. I need to head back to the station tonight, but you call me if you need anything all right?" It's not a question.

"All right."

He takes my chin in one hand and presses his lips against mine. I let him. I let his softness soak in, and I let him take some of the pounding from my chest. The moment lasts a second too short, and my lips are left alone once more. Maybe the decision will be more complicated than I thought.

Kye turns and walks away.

Instead of lying down, I take advantage of my free water. I take the longest shower I have ever had in my life. I am not sure how long I am in there, but the guilt behind it is overwhelming. I finally step out to hear the phone ringing. I get there just in time to hear the dial tone on the other end. According to the keypad on the wall, I have missed eight calls. I'm not sure I have ever received that many calls in my entire life. Ever. I cannot do anything about it, so I leave the phone hanging on the wall and head to my room to get dressed.

I'm barely done before the phone starts up again. My heart stops when I step foot in the kitchen. My front door is wide open, the outside air cold on my skin.

"Do you regret leaving with me?"

The question lingers in the space around us. I look up at the sky and see the stars for the first time in my life. They dance up there. And I can't pick one to look at. My mind can hardly wrap around the idea of there being so many.

"How dare you ask such a question. I mean look at how far we have come. Look at the sky and imagine giving this up."

"But we should be there by now. I've gotten us lost, and I don't know how to reconcile that."

He turns his weight onto his side, no longer looking up at the sky, but softly runs his fingers through the dirt. And all he finds is dirt.

Chapter 24

Three men have found their way into my home. One sits at the bar stool adjacent to where I stand. His cold black eyes match his attire from head to toe. His hair is greased back and shines like the glare on the black windows behind him. Night crept in with this man.

Another man dressed in black stands in front of my mantel, staring me down like the one sitting on the stool nearest me. This one's eyes are as cold, but he has a slight smirk on his face. The third does not look at me and leaves me with only the view of the back of his balding head. He is facing the opposite direction, arms outstretched on the couch. Leaving his apprehension at the door, he's obviously made himself feel at home. He is the one who speaks. Even with his back turned to me, he knows when I approach. He is the only one who speaks.

The phone continues to ring behind us.

"I wouldn't answer that if I were you." His accent is thick, and I can't place it. He is slow in his words, with the consonants barely audible.

I would have to cross in front of the greased-up man to grab the phone, which seems like a risky move altogether. I stay where I am. The phone continues to ring.

"Come sit by me, my dear."

He lights a cigar with a match and continues to face the fireplace and the wall in front of me.

"No," I say.

"Fine. Stay where you are if you wish."

The phone continues to ring.

Contemplating my options, I don't feel like I have many. Three against one, and the men are double my size. I could bolt. But where would I go? If I am caught outside on my first day of house arrest, I'm not sure anyone would even bother to listen to my reason. I'm not ready to be kicked out. I need to prepare. I need a plan first. I could barricade myself in my bedroom. But how long would it be before they broke the door down or came in through the window? Maybe I should just walk in front of Mr. Grease Head and answer the phone. That way, I could at least scream for help.

The phone stops ringing.

Smoke rises above the man's head as he speaks. He turns his head to look at me. "Now, my dear, I need you to come with me."

"No," I say again. "I'm on house arrest. I can't leave the house." And I don't trust you. I don't know who you are, what you want, and no way in hell am I leaving this house with you.

He slowly stands up but continues puffing on his cigar. The room smells like aged firewood. As he turns, I finally see his entire face. His eyes droop. His mouth is shaped into a permanent frown, and his big belly hangs over his pants' buckle. He stops directly in front of my face. His big belly presses against mine. He blows smoke into my face and takes another puff of his cigar. I hold my breath, refusing to cough the smoke.

"Do I look like a man who cares about a house arrest?" he says.

I'm quickly running out of options. "No. No, I suppose not."

"So let's go, my dear," he states.

My feet stay planted to the floor. All I can think about is the smoke that surrounds me. I don't know what to do.

I obviously stand there thinking for too long. The other two men charge me. My arms are pulled behind my back. I kick and squirm and attempt to avoid their grasp. I don't scream, but a monstrous moan I don't recognize escapes my throat.

My arms are tied tightly in an awkward position. Now, I curse and scream. A thick rope is pulled around my head and into my mouth, muting the words and screams. I drop to the floor and make it as difficult as possible for these men to take me. I am picked up off the floor and draped over Mr. Grease Head's shoulder.

The darkness surrounds us the moment they walk out the front door. I am thrown into a vehicle, but I have no idea what it looks like. I don't even know what color it is. All I see is an upside-down view of my house.

As the door to the car shuts, and the engine starts up, I force myself to sit up. Although dark, I can see well enough to take scope of my surroundings. The backseat is larger than anything I have ever seen. Five people could lay down on the floor and still have room for more. Two rows of seats covered in leather are placed at opposite ends—a glass covering hides the driver from the rest of the car. Mr. Accent sits on the opposite side of me and continues to smoke his cigar. Without a window cracked, the smoke makes me dizzy in a matter of minutes.

We drive long enough that my back aches and my hands cramp

behind my back. We take so many turns, I am having a hard time figuring out whether we have left Zone Three or if the driver is just circling to confuse me. I try to squeeze my hands out of their ties, but I am disappointingly unsuccessful.

When we finally stop driving, Mr. Accent puts out his cigar in a plastic cup. He steps out of the car, saying nothing to me.

I remain in the dark by myself for what seems like hours. It makes me think about how repetitious this day has become. The tie on my wrists hurts. My mouth is dry and hurts from the binding. I'm hungry. I can't remember if I have eaten today.

My self-pity is interrupted by the click of a lock. Interior lights brighten the car, and the door opens. A businessman steps in and sits next to me. He seems tall enough to be out of place in the oversized backseat, and he crouches as he moves. He wears a black jacket with a button-down shirt that exposes a slender frame filled with power. His slacks are pressed. His face is freshly shaven. Obviously rich. Maybe mid-fifties.

"My, my, my, Sara, I am so sorry." He gently pulls the rope off my head and out of my mouth. He unties my wrists. Although his actions are kind, there is something about his eyes that screams untrustworthiness. I want to pull away, run or smash open the window and climb out of this damn car. Yet, all I can do is hide my inside panic and outwardly appear calm.

"I am sorry to have done this to you tonight, but I have a large problem, and I need your help."

He leans into me and rubs my wrists as I had done seconds ago. His touch makes the blood in my veins crawl deeper inside my soul.

"And you couldn't just ask?"

"No. You see, your friend Joshua Lorenzo came to see me today."

Instantly I know who this man is. This is the man Janson saw on his last night here on earth. This is the man who killed him. The same man who must be Josh's boss. He is the owner of Water Systems, Inc.

"He talked about you. And this dreadful store you own."

He laughs to himself. He laughs at me and my store. My hands begin to clench.

"And Joshua actually thought that he was making small talk. Probably buying my pity for you and your desperate need to escape from your depression." The laugh grows louder, echoing off the car's black windows.

He places his hand over his chest and finally stops rubbing my wrists. Taking two obvious deep breaths, he continues. "The point is, Sara, that Joshua is a valuable member of my team. I need him. And I need his skill. Josh has maintained the company as a valuable player in government control. I can't chance him walking away from me. I feel as though you might be inhibiting his choices. Despite his meekness, he manages to keep me in control of the government with the one thing they think they have control over."

"Is he okay?" My question comes out in a croaky whisper.

"Of course, he is, my stupid girl. I just told you I need him."

"What do you want from me?" I say.

"That is the easy part. I need you to warn him. As simple as that. Let him know that leaving the company or tearing apart the work he has created is not an option. Make sure he figures out a way to get those bloody cops off his back. He's a smart man. I have full confidence that he can figure it out."

He takes my hands back in his and holds them as if we have been lifelong friends. "Can you do this for me, Sara?"

"Why didn't you just warn him yourself?" I say.

"Oh, I assure you that I did, in fact, speak with him. But I am willing to bet he will listen to you over me. Wouldn't you agree?"

"That's all you want me to do? Warn him?"

"Yes, my dear. That is all. I am a very powerful man. I intend to keep things under control. Lucky for you, I think you are the key. Now, if you would be so kind." He opens the door to the car and motions for me to step out of the vehicle.

Hesitantly, I move past him and take in my surroundings. We stand about fifteen meters away from the Code Enforcement Office. I see exactly what I am meant to just left of the main entrance. Fluorescent light escapes from clear glass windows where two men are arguing at a table in a small room. Josh stands up and paces the room. Kye stands in response and dramatically raises both hands into the air, pleading and frustrated.

I look around the Code Office, and I know it is past curfew. The streets are empty, enveloped in darkness. Neither I nor the man next to me can be seen. The Code Office has an ample number of people walking around inside, but none look past the steps. The emptiness that surrounds me is astonishing.

Mr. Boss Dude motions for me to move towards the large building in front of us. "Go ahead now. You're free."

"I'm on house arrest. I will be removed from all Clean Zones if I walk in there," I whisper.

"I assure you, Sara. You will not be removed from any Clean Zone tonight."

Moments ago, I was terrified of this man. Hours ago, I was scared of his friends. Now, I find myself afraid to leave his side. With no other options, I step one foot in front of the other and move away from the car. With my insides bristling, I walk towards the enforcement building. I keep my eyes glued on the two men arguing in the room ahead of me. With each step I take, I contemplate what I will say when I finish walking up the steps. I need to come up with an excuse for being out. And I need to come up with it quickly.

I hear the engine of the car behind me start up. I turn to see Josh's boss, the creator of Water Systems Inc, still standing there in his pressed suit, leaning up against the car and watching my every move. That's what I will tell them. Exactly the truth. Kind of. Three men broke into my house. I was scared, so I ran straight here. I turn and continue walking. The cigar smell in my house should be proof enough.

My hope falters the moment I hear the gunshot.

"Tommy, we aren't lost. We are precisely where I want to be. My dreams have always been to be at your side regardless of waves crashing down on us. I wouldn't trade a moment of any of this. Not the cold nights sleeping free under the sky, not the nights that hunger weighs on us like a ton of bricks, or even the fear of you never finding your salty water.

"I lay here with you in this moment, and all I can think about is how warm your chest feels when I lay upon it. How it mimics the feel of the rain falling on our cheeks in a time when no one thought it could be done.

"I think of us seeing grass for the first time, fields of it, the stars spanning the sky, and flowers. Just like the ones you place in my hair after a long day's walk. I think of you, Tommy. I think of the way you stretch and moan as you wake up in the morning. I think of the way you look up at the sky to breathe in the afternoon air. How you tilt your head back when you laugh, and how the right side of your mouth curls up slightly each time you're about to tell a joke. I think about how much I love you. So, no. No, I don't regret it. I would do it again and again in every lifetime I am ever lucky enough to have with you: ocean or no ocean. You're the reason my heart beats. You make my heart happy."

Chapter 25

All injuries and illnesses must be reported to local government offices.

I never thought a person could be in so much pain. The antagonizing torture that flows through my veins immobilizes me. I feel it in my chest first. The force of it hits the center of my ribcage with so much potency I scream out as I hunch to ease the impact. The pain moves to my eyes. They glaze over as tears begin to drop. One by one, they are the only thing that helps take the focus off the pain in my chest.

I stumble forward knocking into the cement monument standing before me. Falling to my knees, all I can do is stare at the shadow of the enforcement station. I want to scream. I want to moan out in pain and cry that it had all been a mistake. But all I can do is cry silent tears. Silent tears that mean nothing to any of them.

I did this to myself. I should have known better. Everything was fine before. I was fine. Content in my sheltered world of misjudgment and simplicity. Walling up emotions that I refused to feel and distancing myself from anything that might bring a flicker of reality to my door. I never wanted to be happy. Without happiness, the pain would not be so real and would not penetrate my heart when disaster struck.

I lean closer to the ground, and I hear their feet coming towards me at a run. My eyes are too heavy to open, but I know they are there. Someone is yelling, making frantic demands that I can't understand. I raise my hand to my chest and feel the warm blood trickling through my fingertips.

I have been waiting for this day. Praying for it even. I always thought knowing this life would come to an end would provide me with comfort. That one day, I would be with Tommy again. I could see my mom, my dad, and even Meredith. But I can't let go of the fear—the fear of what happens when I'm gone. I had just started to figure everything out. I had just begun to understand.

My mother is calling for me. My dad is reaching out his hand. I'm searching through the crowd around me, but I can't see him. I'm delirious in desperation. Tommy should be here. He should be waiting for me. Searching past the crowd, I'm drawn to the steps leading up to the building in front of me. I sigh the minute our eyes meet.

Tommy sits with his elbows resting on his knees. Calm. Relaxed. Maybe even a little sad. He ignores the people rushing to get out of the building to help the poor girl lying in front of the steps.

God, I have missed him so much. My heart aches for him.

He shakes his head at me while keeping his eyes locked on mine. "Not yet, Princess," are the words I read from his lips, and everything stops. I don't understand. He continues to signal "no" as more tears fall from my face. I want to run to him, but my body is a stone covered in despair. I close my eyes. I try to convince myself to move.

Someone is whispering to me, holding my head in both hands as if forcing me not to die. I try so hard to open my eyes and see who it is. I try to push past the darkness. I force my eyelids open, weighed down by hundreds of pounds of raging confusion. And then I see him, with Tommy's shadow no longer on the steps behind him. And for the first time in years, I don't want to die.

"Sara, do you want to get up and get something to eat, or do you want to keep sleeping?" Tommy says.

"I'm too tired to move. Maybe in a little bit," I say.

"All right, Princess, sweet dreams."

Chapter 26

No citizen may plant or grow vegetation without a permit.

I wake up in a dark room; handcuffed to the bed rail. The room smells of stale cleaning supplies mixed with lemon. It's funny how my life comes dangerously close to the end, yet I wake up criticizing the room's smell. It's not how my wrists bend on the rusted cuffs that angers me. It's not the raging pain in my chest left over from the bullet meant for me. It's the smell. I am mad about the damn smell. Fresh flowers would do wonders in such an overwhelming environment. Water laws should not matter if this is a dream. Would it kill them for a freaking flower vase?

Josh lays humped over the side of my bed, grasping my free hand in his sleep. The hair on his forehead has fallen onto his face, covering his eyes. I squeeze his hand to make sure this is real.

"Hey, Princess. How are you doing?"

Groggy and lethargic, he sits up and moves closer to me. Although the edge in his voice is evident, he tries hard to hide it.

"I didn't mean to wake you," I whisper.

"Princess, I am so sorry. I am so, so, sorry."

His voice is soft. Remorseful. A full whisper. I have never seen this side of him. His demeanor startles me, and for a moment, I forget why I am here. All I can do is look at him. I don't know how he slept with the beeping heart monitor secured to the wall behind me. I try so hard to ignore it and focus. But instead, I count the beeps in rhythm.

He grabs my hand and kisses it. His eyes are wet. "I am so, so, sorry."

"I was supposed to die, Josh," I whisper.

"Shhh…"

Tears fill his eyes as the upper half of his body moves onto the bed with me, hovering close but careful not to put any pressure on me. "I couldn't stop it. God knows I tried. You have to tell the cops what happened." His words are rushed. Urgent. "Tell them everything."

"Stop."

It hurts my chest to raise my voice above a whisper, but the darkness in the room tells me I should be whispering at this hour of the night. "Stop and listen." I push him backward with my free arm and urge him to sit in the chair at the side of the bed. "This pity thing you've got going on doesn't suit you well." I squeeze his hand in my own, begging him to understand. "I need you to go home and get the bag under my bed. Grab three pairs of fresh clothes for me. Vitamin packs, as many food rations as you can. At least four bottles of water. Utensils. Soap. Matches. Don't forget the matches. A knife. A compass. Something to collect rainwater. Bleach. And those two blankets I have folded over the chair in the living room. Do the same thing for yourself."

"Sara …"

"Take both bags about three miles south of the west gate. Throw them over the fence. There is enough shrubbery there that they should be hidden until we need them."

The more I talk, the more my chest hurts.

"No," is all he says.

"I'm either gone, or you're dead. The option is no longer yours. Pull your stubborn head out of your ass and look at this logically. If I'm to survive out there, I need you to come with me, and I need the stuff to ensure I can do it." I squeeze his hand even harder. "If I am thrown out, I can't do it alone." I gasp for breath. "If I stay, you can't guarantee that it will be with you…"

He stares at me without words, his eyes are hard. I can't read them. "And the picture of Tommy. Grab that, too."

Josh does not move. His hardened eyes press into mine as if it pains him. Finally standing up, he kisses my forehead and walks to the door. Saying nothing else, he leaves.

I have no idea what he is going to do.

I watch the door close behind him and my mind wrestles with itself. Am I wrong? Is there another choice? Was I too stern with him after he tried sharing his guilt and sorrow? The meandering thoughts make me crazy. Ironically, the nuisance beeps lull me back to sleep.

When I wake up once more, the night has passed. It's no longer the smell of cleaning supplies that fills my nose. It's no longer Josh who I see when I wake up. Instead, Senator Frank Lorenzo sits on the small sofa that rests under the window. The smell of egocentric arrogance fills my nose.

"What do you want?" I say.

"Hello to you, too."

"What do you want?" I say again.

"I want you to tell me what happened. I want you to tell me what the hell I should do with you," he says.

"I don't know what happened. And I'm not under your keep anymore. It shouldn't be your problem." My chest hurts. The pain is so vivid it feels like I am being shot all over again.

"Five days ago, you were placed on house arrest. And that same day you show up near death on the curb of one of my stations. With all due respect, sweetheart, you are a very big problem."

"I don't know what happened. I want a doctor. Now get out."

"Tommy was a jerk of a kid. And even he had a better bedside manner than you."

"Tommy loved you! And all you ever did was push him away!"

The screams tear at my insides and force my trembling free hand to grip the rail on the bed. Years of pent-up anger are trying to sneak out. "He was the only thing that kept people in that damn house going for as long as we did! It's because of you he is dead! All of them! They are all dead because of you!"

"If anything was because of me, it was that I allowed a pathetic orphan to live under my roof and spoil the outlook my boys should have had on life." Calm and collectively, he stands up and swaggers to my side. "My dear child…" He tries to reach for my hand, just as I pull it away. It lands on the pounding rise and fall of my chest.

"I'm not your child; I'm not even your blood!" I can't stop the tears once they come. The sobs make the pain even worse.

"They are all dead because of *you* … both my boys included." He leans over the bedrail closer to my face.

"Both your boys aren't dead, in case you've forgotten. Josh lives in the same godforsaken town as you do. Just because you ignore him doesn't make him dead!"

"You misunderstood." He pulls his hand back and straightens up, sweeping the wrinkles out of his shirt. "I'm doing everything I can for Josh, whether he understands it or not. You think it's a coincidence he left you and Tommy just days before meeting Janson Thomas? Josh needed some clarity in his life, so I found a way to support him."

He walks to the door and turns his head back to me one last time. "I'm keeping Josh safe as best as I can. But just like Tommy, I can't always be there for every mishap. Unfortunately, there is nothing else I can do for him."

"You're sentencing him to death!"

"No, no. Those are all his own choices." He opens the door and lets it slam behind him.

I cry myself to sleep, hoping the conversation was a dream, hoping with every breath I have left that Frank is wrong and Josh will be okay. Hoping it all was not my fault.

When I wake up again, it's a full room I see: two nurses, one doctor, Josh, Kye, and another enforcement officer. I don't know how they all made their way into my room. The doctor is poking and prodding at me. The nurse is right at his side.

"Ms. Carson? Ms. Carson? My Name is Dr. Yangish. Can you tell me what day it is?" he says as he continues to poke and prod me.

"No. No, I can't."

"Can you wiggle your fingers for me? Good. Now your toes. Good. Ms. Carson, you have a bullet wound dangerously close to your spine. You must limit your movements for now. Do you understand?"

"Can I get the cuff removed? It's hurting my arm."

The doctor looks to the enforcement officer.

The officer nods. "Only temporarily." He moves to free my wrist.

"This button right here is for pain," the doctor says. "This one is for a nurse." He turns and directs his next comments to the others in the room with me. "Make it as brief as possible. She must rest." The doctor and the two nurses walk out of the room.

Kye and the unknown officer move to both sides of my bed and sit down. Their movements are rigid and mechanical. Josh moves to sit on the sofa behind Kye. This is obviously not a social visit.

"Are you in pain?" Kye says.

I nod in response.

We sit in silence for what seems like several minutes. His uniform tells me he is on duty. Even the way he sits, with his hands cupped on his lap, screams work-related, but the look in his eyes is contradictory. He does not want to be working. He does not want to be here for work. The unknown officer clears his throat. Kye looks in his direction briefly, then back at me once more.

"Sara, we need to know what happened," Kye says.

My eyes move to Josh. He sits on the sofa with his head down, looking between his feet. He looks up to meet my eyes once he realizes I haven't answered the question.

"Sara, it is essential you tell us what happened," Josh says.

I continue to look past Kye, hoping for some help from Josh. I want to know if he did as I asked. I want to know how much wiggle room I have. His eyes look so sad.

"Sara. Sara, do you remember what happened?" Kye says.

My eyes slowly move back to Kye. The small action alone tells him I do.

"Can you tell us what happened?"

My eyes remain glued to his, yet my mouth remains closed.

"Sara, unless you talk, your citizenship will be terminated. You must talk to us." He pauses. "Talk to me." His eyes look as sad as Josh's.

Sorrow doesn't suit him well—either one of them. I was the one who was shot and yet I feel I am holding up better than both these men.

It's only a place. I don't understand why they can't see that. I lived. Bottom line. Who really cares if I live inside or outside those stupid gates? If there is one thing I have learned over the past few weeks, it's that emotions come and go no matter where a person is. They can't be stopped. The pain of the past, or the optimism the future holds, it's the people who matter most in life. It's making damn sure they are protected from harm. I couldn't protect Tommy. I'm not making that mistake again. If Kye and Josh could both see hope for Austin, why can't they see that hope for me?

Kye slowly shifts in his seat as if moving as close to my bed as possible. My eyes meet his.

"I was shot. I was shot, and then…" I stop to take a breath, trying not to say too much. "Frank came." My eyes plead with Josh.

His eyes snap open, and he leans forward, his body in panic.

"He was telling me about how he helped you get your job."

"That doesn't sound much like him." His voice is low, talking to only me even though the room is filled with other people. "It almost makes him sound noble."

"It was more about control. Controlling you because he could never control Tommy. But…" I close my eyes and swallow. "Frank was never my guardian angel. He's yours…" I feel the drugs they pumped into me suffocating my every thought. The tears start down my face, and my head moves to the filled chair next to me. "Kye, please. Please let this wait. Can't I at least sleep it off?"

"Sara, I wish I could, but no. We need a statement."

Filled with pain and panic, I am unsure what to do with myself other than breathe. Josh has never been one to prepare. Our whole lives, he just did things without thinking. I sure as hell hope he pulled through for me. If he didn't, I am not sure what my future holds. I don't know what I will do.

The nurses come in with Niles at their side. They change a few IVs and bandages, but I am so groggy I am not sure I am focusing on anything except all the men in my room waiting for me to talk.

"Ms. Carson, we are done waiting. Your time is up. We need to know what happened." Niles' voice is stern. Father-like.

I stare at him, feeling like the blood is draining from my face. "I remember my house being broken into. I remember running to the station for help. But that is all I remember." The statement is directed towards Niles. If I were to look at anyone else in the room, I am quite positive my voice would falter, and even Niles would know I am lying. Even now, the room is silent.

I can feel Josh's eyes on me, hard and cold, almost angry. Kye seems devastated. Sad eyes that scream sorrow and shock. The unknown officer seems confused as though wondering why Niles hasn't continued to question me about the break-in. But Niles, the bastard who probably had it out for me from the very beginning, smiles.

"Is that all you would like to tell us, Ms. Carson?" He smirks as he talks to me.

"Yes, that's it. I'm sorry, but I don't remember anything else."

"This is ridiculous!" Josh jumps up from the couch. He clenches his fists as he screams out. "Sara, they are going to revoke your citizenship." His face turns red, and he points to the window. "People die out there, Sara! You know that better than anyone! And this time, you will do it with a bullet wound to the chest. This isn't a game!" He turns to Niles. "If she won't talk, I will. I'll tell you exactly what happened to her and why. Anything and everything you want to know. From the beginning. All of it." He no longer points towards the window. His finger is now directed at me.

All three officers in the room look back and forth from each other. Silence finds the room once more.

"Okay. Mr. Lorenzo. Tell us what we want to know." Niles' smirk fades. He was not expecting this.

"No. Not here. She gets to stay here in peace and recover from a bullet wound that almost killed her, and I get one more cup of coffee in the cafeteria before you whisk me off to punishment." Josh's voice remains calm yet stern. "That's my offer."

The other men look around the room, trying to feel each other out.

Niles responds. "Fine."

Josh glances at me without coldness. "The option is no longer yours."

All four men walk out of my room. Kye is the only one to turn and look back. Even through my grogginess, I know I am helpless.

"Tommy! Tommy! Wake up! Please, God, wake up. Please."

My hand passes down his cheek, humid from sweat, sticky from illness.

"Tommy, I need you to wake up. We aren't at the ocean yet, and you promised to take me to the ocean."

His hair lay matted against his skin, his lips dry to the touch. "Please, Tommy. Please. I need you."

Chapter 27

Irrigation rights are reserved for Water System Inc. and strictly prohibited for private citizens.

I spend the next few hours in my room in silence, circling my thumbs around each other over and over again. I pump myself full of morphine a few times and then second guess it. I can't help but wonder if I am trying to dull the pain in my chest or the pain in my mind.

I know that boss of Josh's will kill him for talking. He had Janson killed for something far less intentional than ratting out the company. The thought crosses my mind that he might be the crazy son of a bitch who trained Janson to steal water in the first place.

I'm not sure what the government will do to Josh. Sure, he might be cleared of all murder suspicions, but they treat their water laws with more status. Stealing water has been punishable with death since before I was born. I would put my money on a public hanging if I had to guess. The real question is who will want to have him killed first.

Kye and Josh are the only men to return. Quietly, they both have a seat on the sofa next to each other. Several minutes pass. I gawk at them when I can't handle it anymore. "For goodness' sake, will one of you just tell me what happened!"

Kye leans forward with his elbows resting on his knees and his lips pressed tightly together. Josh raises his eyebrows, but otherwise, he remains expressionless, slouched on the sofa, his arms crossed at his chest.

"Josh is under my watch until Niles gets back," Kye says. "Niles went to talk to the captain at the station so we can figure out our next move." He gestures with his thumb to Josh. "Genius over here spilled quite a story in a cafeteria filled with innocent ears which could hear every detail. People began to scatter as soon as they realized what he was saying might actually be true."

Josh smiles slightly. His smile runs deep into his eyes.

A heavy knock on the door interrupts Kye. A plump nurse wearing white from head to toe enters. She flips through her chart before noticing us in the room.

"Sorry, boys, but find some other place to gossip. I need to clean up my patient. Ms. Carson, my name is Ida. I will be helping you today."

"We'll be waiting right outside," Kye mumbles as they are pushed out the door.

Ida loses little time. As soon as they leave, she takes out my IVs and starts to check my bandages. She tapes and secures a fresh bandage over the stitches etched into the right of my chest.

Not only does she manage to give me clean sheets, but she cleans me top to bottom as well. By the time she is done with me, I am free of all IVs and monitors. I still hurt like hell. Maybe even more than before. I was hoping for a few more days on an IV as my crutch.

I grunt and groan in pain each time she moves me. I try to hold it in and act brave, but really, who would I be acting for? The doctor told me not to move. Yet here I am, being bent in ways I'm not sure I could have done even before a near spinal injury.

"How's about I help you to the washroom?" she says.

"Yes, please," I say between gritted teeth. They are cleaning me up just to kick me out.

She helps me up and stabilizes my wobbly body. "Exhale each time your foot changes pressure points."

She puffs her cheeks and bulges her eyes as I do the exact opposite. My exhales come out as whimpers.

Helping me out of bed is excruciating, but nothing compared to the long walk to the end of the room. Every breath, tears at the stitches holding me together. She escorts me into the bathroom and turns her back to give me some privacy.

"Have you heard them rumors yet, Ms. Carson?" she says.

"No. No, I haven't. Rumors about what?"

"Well, my oh my, do I have a lot to catch you up on." Touching her arm softly, I signal to her I am ready for more of her help. She walks me over to the sink.

"Rumor has it the government has been hiding water from us. The whole thing turns out to be a scam. We've been rationing our water for nothing. Truth is, they have plenty. So much that they could even open them gates to the outsiders and still have enough that we wouldn't need no rations. Just thinking about it makes me sick. Them poor babies so thirsty they have nothing to drink. Nothing to clean their stink. Nothing to cook their food. And for what? I tell you, it ought to be that stinking senator. I had a bad feeling about him since he was elected. I just don't get it. I just don't get it."

"What would the government have to do with it? Isn't Water Inc. a separate entity?"

"Oh, darlin', please. Think about it. The government controls everything. What you eat, how much you eat, when you get to go, and when you get to stay. They gots to be the ones behind the whole thing! Why else would this be happening? My friend Betsy was getting sick a whiles back. The only thing she could hold down was water. Ran through her rations in a quarter of the time she should have. But once her water was off, she got worse. The health inspectors showed up, but her dada hid her in the rafters of his house. She was barely holding onto life. Dehydrated with illness beyond anything I have ever seen. It's a miracle them health inspectors never found her. Turns out she had been so thirsty all the time 'cuz she was with child. She lost that baby in her dehydration. Poor, poor thang. Water would have saved it. God knows water would have saved it."

Turning the sink off, she reaches for a towel for my hands. "The minute she heard 'bout them hoarding water, she walked off her shift. I never. Said she's going out to tells as many as she could. She be trying to start a protest. Maybe even riots. Her at the head."

Helping me walk out of the washroom, she continues talking. "I don't know 'bout you, honey. But I be mad. Very mad. Them bastards could control our minds, and I bet ya it still wouldn't be 'nough for 'em. Selfish. Selfish. Selfish."

Her thoughts are interrupted by a bang outside the window. It vibrates the glass and reminds me of the sound of gunshots. A sound that recently tore through my chest. The crack is so loud that it makes my body cringe, and the seizing in my chest starts again.

Ida pulls me to the window to see the cause of the noise. The sight outside the window is astonishing. People flood the streets.

Screaming. Arguing. Fistfights and objects are being thrown through every window in view.

Cowering away from the window, we both sit on the edge of the bed. I can't help but be grateful we are on the second floor, yet I am apprehensive at the same time. It looks like a war zone out there.

Just as Kye and Josh barge into the room, alarms sound behind them.

Josh pushes a wheelchair into the room with him. "Sorry, Ida, but it's time to go."

"Mmm, hmm. I do say so."

She walks out of the room without another word, shaking her head as she goes. Josh helps me into the wheelchair, and he throws an empty bag toward Kye.

"Grab everything you can. Anything you can find. Antibiotics, pain relievers, alcohol, bandages. Anything and everything that may be useful."

To my surprise, Kye does not argue with Josh's commands and heads out to salvage whatever closet he can find. Josh helps move me onto the wheelchair and follows close behind. To my dismay, the halls are empty. Ida's stories must be more than rumors if this is the after-effect of Josh's contribution to the day's events.

The three of us roll out the front doors in a matter of minutes. The streets are full of people taking their anger out on anyone they think might be worth it. They are reacting instead of thinking things through and finding the real cause of their anger. They act more like ravaging animals than humans.

I finally dare to ask, "Where are we going?"

No one answers me.

"We need the Jeep," Kye says.

We stay to the side of the crowd and push our way through.

Kye at the head, he leads Josh. Helpless, I grasp the bag in my lap.

Up ahead, I finally see it. The same statue that just days prior I lay bleeding on. This is the place where we finally stop.

Dozens of uniformed cops march out of the front doors and down the station's steps in clean, solid lines. With batons and guns raised, they rush ahead—their path curves towards us. We wait. Motionless. Waiting.

Niles stops in front of us. "Joshua Lorenzo. You are under arrest for breaking Water Laws one, two, three, and four. There will be no jury for your crimes."

He ignores the crowds and rioting surrounding us. His steps are purposeful, his voice condemning.

Josh turns and bends down to me before Niles finishes talking. Pulling me into an embrace, he presses his lips against my left temple. "Both bags are exactly where you wanted them. Get out before it gets dark." He pushes his mouth against mine. "Don't you dare wait for me."

"Wait. No! Josh! They can't do this! It's not your fault!"

I pull myself out of the wheelchair and try to stumble toward him. My hands barely brush past his, and I fall to my knees. Enforcements grab him and pull him away from my grasp. They cuff both hands behind his back.

Kye grabs my arms before I crash into the ground. He keeps me upright and pulls me into a stand. My weight is anchored on his core. He pulls me backward, away from Josh and Niles. My legs swing at the wheelchair to get it out of my way. I strain to reach Josh.

"Get her out of here, Kye!" Josh is calm. The patrol forces him towards the front steps of the building.

"Josh! No! You can't do this! It's not happening without you! I won't do it!" Tears pour down my face. I try to stumble towards him, adrenaline in my veins pushing me forward.

His eyes lock on mine, whispering the words that scream and bleed into my heart. "I trust him, Sara."

"No! Please! No!"

"I love you."

Josh's words come out eerily calm as an officer clips him in the back of the head. His body goes limp.

I fall to the ground with him, even though we are several meters apart.

Kye grabs my arms, and he pulls me into a standing position. Blood splatters across the pavement. I'm not sure whose. Mine? Or Josh's?

"We have to go, Sara. We have to go now."

He hauls me backward as I sob. I turn my head just as Josh's limp body is dragged up the steps.

I don't remember how I sat back into the chair, how we moved into the thick of the crowd, or how my head ended up between my knees. We head for the side of the building. I look up at the sound of gunshots in the street next to us. This time it's not rioting citizens begging for freedom, begging for more water. It's armed enforcement shooting at anyone and everyone in the street. Men, women, even young children are being killed for wanting to live out their own lives. Being killed for wanting something that they are never allowed enough of.

Kye pushes me to rows of black Jeeps. He lifts me out of the chair and sets me in the passenger side of a Jeep three rows in. He places a hand on my cheek. "Stay here. I will be right back."

I am left there to cry alone.

My hands cover my mouth as the tears run down my face. I cry for everyone. For myself. For Josh. I cry for my pain inside and out. I can't force myself to stop even as I replay the blow to his head over and over. I pull my hands away from my eyes to wipe them dry on my blood-stained shirt. My blood. My blood drips in front of my eyes. And somehow, that is all it takes before clarity hits me.

This fight started before I was born. It wasn't Josh's fault, and he sure as hell did not deserve his future. But I'll be damned if I don't at least try. We might still have a chance. He might still have a chance.

I have no idea where Kye went, but I feel like I need to be doing something. Anything. I go through the Jeep and find a can of lighter fluid. I push myself out of the car and stumble to the next Jeep. The blood from my chest begins to soak my shirt, but I ignore my pain and focus on preventing any more for Josh. The torn stitches clot into the blood that now drips down my fingers as I move. Drenching the side of the enforcement building with as much lighter fluid as I can, I soak the walls just as the blood soaks my shirt.

Kye enters my line of vision with a wagon full of red containers. "That won't do a damn thing. Save the rest. We're going to need it."

He throws the remaining bottles of lighter fluid into the Jeep and takes a small device out of his pocket. The moment he attaches it to the wall in front of us, it begins to blink. "Get back in the car before you bleed out and kill yourself."

I do as he says without arguing, feeling hopeless. Helpless.

He stacks the back of the Jeep full of what I can only assume is gasoline. He stops to throw a bag to me. "Get a clean bandage. Apply pressure to that wound with whatever you can find." His face is resigned, hiding every emotion emanating from my broken body.

He jumps into the front of the Jeep and starts the car before I find the bandages. To keep from wasting a good bandage, I take a fire blanket from the backseat of the car and push it under my already blood-stained shirt. I hold it to the wound. "Three miles south of the west gate. On the outside. That's where we need to go," I murmur.

"Okay."

He races to the outskirts of town. We are only minutes away from the station when the explosion fills our ears. I don't look. I don't want to know how bad it is. My only hope is that it saved Josh from a torturous death that he did not deserve. Or maybe, just maybe, gave him the chance he needed to get out.

Bodies pave the streets in front of the main gate. There is no one left for the watch guards to shoot as we approach. Kye reaches over me into the glove compartment to pull out a pistol without hesitation. The three guards who refuse to let anyone through are taken out one by one. His calmness should be reassuring. But it's not. Instead, I'm baffled that he is running with me without a second thought. He killed for me. Does he go because he was asked to? Does he go because of me?

We find our way over the bodies of those who tried to escape and drive through the gate.

Once more, I find myself running from a clean zone. This time I won't be allowed back. And this time, I leave without a Lorenzo. All I can do is cry my way back to freedom.

"He's gone, Sara."

Josh sits at the side of my bed, talking to me even though my mind is blank. A stone wall he keeps trying to talk to over and over again.

"If you can't come back to me, then all those good memories of him go, too. There is no one else who shares those memories with us. It's just you and me. We need to keep him alive, Sara, and no one can do that better than you."

Chapter 28

All minors in the protected Clean Zone school systems will

receive a full education, including the history of

water laws and the importance of abiding by water

protection laws.

Within the hour, Kye finds the two bags hidden in the brush. I lay lethargic in the front seat of the Jeep, begging my dazed brain to remain conscious. I am aware enough to guide him, but his control over the situation is remarkable. He listens to my directions and follows without question.

Within that same hour, the sky around us fills with smoke. We can't drive fast enough away from the ash falling from the sky like snow, desperately trying to distance ourselves from the newly created war zone. The Jeep dips into crevasses, climbs over broken tree limbs, and tumbles over broken slabs of pavement. Every jarring bump in the road tears my sutures open.

Kye sees the pain on my face and slows the car down as much as possible. "We can't keep going like this. We need to find a place to stop. A place where you can heal," he says.

"Maddox. We need to find Maddox," I say.

"Tell me how, Sara."

I search my brain, but all I find is emptiness and confusion. I feel dizzy, remembering the last time I was outside the gates or the last time Tommy and I found Maddox. Or the time when a new friendship blossomed with Kye, and I lost Austin. I remember a cabin in the middle of a field. Not shielded. Not hidden, but a stark statement daring anyone to come get him. But I don't think that was Maddox. That was Tommy. To get to Maddox, we need to find the gas station.

Maddox will help me. He will help us.

Kye veers the Jeep to the side and waits for more direction. Waits for my thoughts to uncloud. He pulls the Jeep into a brush thicket. We are hidden by the descending darkness and the remains of an old highway.

He tilts my seat back and pulls the blood-covered fire blanket off my chest. I know what he sees. The pain is bad enough. I can only imagine what it looks like. He apologizes as he pulls my shirt off, leaving me in a blood-covered undergarment and nothing more.

I grimace in pain as he pours cool liquid over my freshly opened bullet wound. My vision becomes blurry. The twinkling of the stars I see across his face, the fear and the determination blur together. I know it's not my determination, but his strength radiates toward me.

I never saw Kye as someone who would walk away with me or pour life back into my chest, or stitch thread in and out of a bullet wound. He has always been the enforcement cop who is dirty and working for the awful government I hate with all my being. At least the part of me that is still pieced together properly.

I know how he feels, and I have for a while now, but today I actually see it. He left everything. His home, his precious job, his responsibility. For me.

As he works on stitching me up, I try so hard to think of nothing else but him. How his face wrinkles up in the bright sun, how his head drops when opening the door for me, and even his calm resolve. He ignores my screams as he works. I try so hard to keep my eyes open, to stare at his stupid-ass dimple that has found its way into my heart.

"Four miles north of the main gate, there is an old gas station. We have to get to Maddox. He is the only one who can help," I say between gritted teeth.

"Okay. Okay. As soon as we can move you. That is exactly where we will go."

I blackout.

I wake up in the backseat with a fresh top on, fresh bandages, and a clean fire blanket folded neatly over my legs and torso. I try and sit up even though I probably should not move. How many times must a person nearly die before common sense starts to kick in?

The night is dark, but I can see Kye sitting on the Jeep's hood. His hunched-over back faces me. I imagine his face is filled with sorrow. His regret is clear in the way his shoulders lean forward. But then I see something so powerful; I manage to forget my pain. Forget my guilt or selfish fears.

I see him. Not what he presents to the world. But him. His head leans back, and he looks at the sky. He sees the billions and billions of stars for what must be the first time in his life. His shoulders relax. His shoulders do not hold impending doom, fear, or even regret. It's of peace.

I lay down and allow him to have his moment in privacy. With everything that has happened, it's the least I can do.

With everything that has happened, do I have peace?

"There are many different ways to love, Sara."

Dr. Hammid's glasses slip down the bridge of her nose. Too distracted by her concern for me, she does not notice.

"The human body is an amazing machine, but so is the soul, the heart, and the mind. Trust me when I tell you, you have room in your heart for more than one person."

"I don't want to love more than one person. Everyone I love is gone. They are always taken from me like my love is a curse waiting to fill their lives with venom."

"That is not true, and you know it. Their lives were filled with joy—every single one of them. Death does not mean their life was filled with poison. You must separate their lives from their deaths."

"But death took them. Nothing is left."

"Do you honestly believe that? That the thought of them doesn't change the way you behave? That the lessons your parents taught you didn't leave an impact on you? That the love you felt for them doesn't scare you into loving more?"

"It hurts so bad when it's gone."

"But the love isn't gone, Sara. Just because they died doesn't mean they stopped loving you or you them. It doesn't mean you have to stop living, too. It is not love that dies. Love lives on forever."

Chapter 29

Atmospheric water harvesting is not permitted for private residents.

I wake up in a bed in a room far too familiar in my memories. The walls are covered with chipping paint, the floor with a rustic carpet old enough to keep even the mice away. But the blanket on top of me is fresh, and the smell in the air is heavy with oak.

"How long have I been asleep?"

Kye sits at my feet. He places his hand on my forehead, presumably checking for a fever.

"Several days. I gave you a few shots of the morphine we had, another of an antibiotic."

Satisfied with his touch, he leans his head back on the seat. "It's better that you slept. I don't imagine you would have stayed still willingly." Closing his eyes at the thought, he is motionless, apprehensive about touching me any more than necessary. He is treating me like I am made of glass.

"Where is Maddox?" My voice is hoarse.

He reaches for a jug of water stowed at his feet and fills a nearby water bottle. He leans over to help me with a few sips. I oblige. Gratefully.

"Where did the water come from?" I ask.

"There is a water generator out back, plenty hidden, but also plenty full. No one has been here since we arrived. It doesn't look like anyone has been here in a while."

Although I am not surprised, it does make my heart sink.

"I went through all our stuff. It seems you prepared fairly well."

That's all it takes. A quick reminder that half of this stuff wasn't meant for him. "Kye…"

"Sara, you have to believe me when I tell you I didn't know. Any of it. I didn't…" Both his hands move up to cover his face. "I'm sorry."

"Why did you leave, Kye? Why did you choose this side of the fence?"

He runs his fingers through his hair and fixes his gaze on my own. "They lied to everyone. About everything. I mean all those people. For all these years. What role I played. How I acted on their behalf. I never truly realized I was on the wrong side."

"Are you okay?" I say.

"I'm angry. I feel betrayed. But weirdly, I feel kind of better. You made me feel so torn about things, but now there is no question. You're safe now, and that's all that matters."

"And yet you just dropped everything. Everything." My eyes squint at him; my voice is soft.

"What they were doing was wrong." He sits up straighter and hands me the water bottle one more time. "I was fourteen when my dad paid off the senate in Zone One to get me in early. I was recruited at fifteen and pushed through the ranks faster than anyone had ever seen. Through each rank, with every captain or officer, the message was always the same. Protect the people."

He takes a drink from the water bottle. "But they weren't doing that. I didn't sign up to kill innocent people or keep water away from those who needed it. I wanted to protect people. That's what I wanted. To keep them safe." He rests his elbows on his knees and turns back to me. "That's what I was trying to do, keep you safe."

I reach my hand out to his and squeeze it the instant he takes the gesture. "What do we do now?"

"I have absolutely no idea. You're the one who has been out here before. I was hoping you would heal up and take the lead on this one." He grins.

"Have you seen any sign of Austin here?"

"None."

"Help me up?" I say.

He holds me steady as I remember how to move my feet. My wobbling feet take me from the cot tucked tightly into the corner of the room, past the small table in the kitchen, where I open the screen to a door. I take a tentative step outside. What I see takes my breath away.

When I was here last time, it was dark. But now I can see the beauty. The land is no longer devoid of life. Patches of grass cover the ground, and shrubs push up and say hello to the world.

We walk out of the shrubbery, and Kye urges me to have a seat on a nearby tree stump. I let him help me sit without argument, and he hands me an energy bar. We stare into the wilderness.

Although many trees remain bare, several have foliage nesting on their branches and give us hope the land is coming back. The wind whistles through the leaves and ruffles the hair resting on my neck. We eat the bars in silence, his body leaning on the bark to my side. The scruff on his face is a darker brown than the hair on his head and sets off the brilliance of his eyes. He is not afraid. He is never anything but stable, even during the craziness of a storm.

"Do you think Josh is dead?" I say.

He does not answer. Instead, he pulls me in for an embrace. "I should have listened to you in the first place. I am so sorry, Sara."

"You need to stop apologizing. Being an asshole is much more pleasing on you."

We sit in silence for several minutes and enjoy the growing greenery around us and the wind caressing our skin. And even though my body feels torn to pieces, and the ache of loss is nearly tipping me over, I feel at peace right here at this moment. "We need to keep going south. As far as the Jeep can take us," I say.

"We probably have enough gas for a few days. The Jeep will last longer if we stay on old highways the best we can."

"We'll find the best shelter for us, too. How much food do we have?"

"If we're careful, it will last us twice as long as the gas," he murmurs as he gazes at the nature that was never a part of his upbringing. "Every time we see water, we should collect and purify it. That's not something we want to ever get low on."

"Kye…"

Biting my lower lip, my hand touches the back of his neck. "Thank you." Because I can hear it in his voice, he wants this. He's doing this not out of guilt or because of me. He wants to find something better. He sees my dream.

Pursing his lips together, he nods his head slightly. "Not yet, though. You need to prove to me you can move around without bleeding all over the place."

"I assure you, I'm fine."

"So, prove it. We'll scour the place here, see if there's anything useful we can take."

"No. I won't let you do that."

"Why not?" he says.

"This is a safe place. Not just for me but countless others. We can't take that safety away from people just because we don't know them or their situation. Maddox may not be here right now, but that doesn't mean he won't be later. Or others. There is always hope for more."

"Fine. But we still aren't leaving until you can go ten minutes without getting pale and weak at the knees."

"Deal."

"We can stay here, you know. Wait and help people out who come along." Tommy's hand pushes the loose strands of hair behind my ears.

"Isn't that kind of like cheating? Not picking one place or another but staying somewhere in the middle?" I say.

"It's not cheating as long as you make a decision. So what is it, Princess? What is your decision?"

Chapter 30

All citizens must be employed or receive an income by their

high school graduation date.

The soft moonlight dims as I look past the mountains and towards the horizon. Empty eyes filled with sorrow look back at my reflection. I don't know who I am anymore.

I stare out the window at everything. Everything we pass: empty dwellings, fallen trees. But we pass more than just barren landscapes. We pass the land that should have housed more of a population. We pass over the empty roads of a world's past mistakes. When we were locked inside the Clean Zones, it was easy to forget how messed up the world had become. But now, driving through it all, the truth hits us hard. Nothing was left. The abandoned farms were left to nothing but dust. Everything had been lost.

But it can be different for us. I can choose to see a blank slate—an ability to start anew with nothing standing in our way. I can choose to see everything instead of nothing. I can see Kye. Each blink of his eye or twitch of his hand, like he is forcing himself not to reach for me. He is trying. God, I know he is. He gives me space to grieve. He tries to figure things out for himself as I do the same. My eyes glisten with tears as I think of my past, and I cannot help it. Each time it happens, I try so hard to focus on something else, like how his hair falls into his eyes as he stares out the window or how he rubs at his eyes to keep awake.

He is so different from everyone I have ever known.

Not too long ago, he occupied many of my thoughts. Now, with everything that has happened, I have so many other things to worry about. What happens next? How do we move on? Where do we go from here? It feels so great to have hope.

"I used to dream of finding the beach," I say. "Nestling my toes in the sand and listening to the waves crash against the shore."

"What do you mean used to?"

"Tommy died. A lot of my dreams died after that."

"And now? What do you think about dreaming all over again?"

"That sounds like something I am finally willing to do."

"What would you think about including me in that dream? Maybe showing me everything about the beach that you used to see in your dreams? I can be the person you walk with in the sand," he says.

And I think that's what it boils down to. Now that Josh is gone, I feel like I've lost Tommy all over again. He was the one person who held those memories with me. He was the one I could talk to, laugh with, and even mourn with. But was he truly the only one?

"Let me be that person for you," he says.

Kye gazes to the horizon, and that's when I know.

I don't want to replace Tommy or Josh. Either of them. I needed both of them in my life for my own special reasons, and each mattered immensely. I don't want a replacement or a replica. I want something new. I want exactly who Kye is now. Not who he was or what he always wanted to represent. The now.

I clasp his hand in my own as he readjusts the shirt buttons over my new bandage. The back of my fingers run across his cheek, and his eyes lock onto mine. Our lips meet as I lift my body closer to his and pull him in by the back of his neck. Yielding to my embrace, he slides his arms around my upper back, and I arch in response. He pulls back slightly to hold my stare. The rush of emotion feels thick on my face.

"Yes," I say.

"I need you to know. So just listen, okay?"

I blink in agreement. My chest rises and falls in quick submission.

"To me, you're the girl who has faced loss over and over and still triumphed. The girl who is bold enough to let me in even though the entire world told you not to. You were shot in the chest and still tried to blow up the enforcement office with a measly can of lighter fluid." His chest shakes with laughter as he kisses me tenderly once more. "You have nothing but will and determination, but I want you to smile at me. I want you to be glad that I am the one here at your side."

It's as though he's read my thoughts about starting anew. Crinkling my brow, I tilt my head and place both my hands on the sides of his face. "We are here at this very moment because of you, Kye. It makes you look weak if you start questioning that." My gaze falters between his eyes and his lips as I grin. "I much prefer you as an ass."

The right side of his mouth tilts up, and he moves closer to me.

We stare across an empty field. Mountains rise on the horizon to the west, smoky clouds covering their tops. To the east, the land lays flat. North and south are a mixture of both.

Kye gets out of the car and heads towards the mountains, stops, turns in all directions, then begins to walk once more. Confused, I get out and follow. I catch up with him twenty meters out as he nonchalantly places his hands in his pockets, turns towards me, and smiles a crooked smile.

"What's going on?" I say.

"I don't know where I'm going," he says.

Crinkling my eyebrows, I turn and look in all directions as he did moments ago.

"What should we do?" he says.

"You forget I never actually made it anywhere last time I left. I have no idea."

"Well, if we go west, we will need to climb the mountains. I don't know how to get a Jeep through a mountain. East, we will probably hit more mountains. And south, well, I don't know what's South. North is the way we came. We are not going back North."

"Well then, I think it's obvious."

He continues to turn in each direction and stare into the distance.

"Then South. Let's go South," I say.

He turns to look South once more. "Then what? What happens once we get South?"

"We look for others, I suppose."

"And when we find others, what then?" He closes the distance between us. He brushes my cheek with the back of his hand.

"I don't know," I whisper.

"Okay," he whispers back. He drops his hand and kisses me softly on the lips. He walks back to the car.

We climb into the Jeep and head South.

This time as Kye drives, he hums and sings of grace and eternity.

His songs are soft, yet his voice travels over the rocky terrain. He occasionally stops to discuss our gasoline and water supplies or check our route, but his tone has changed from mournful to hopeful. He turns to smile at me occasionally, and later, he reaches for my hand and squeezes it slightly.

"You're being creepy again," I say.

His dimple perks. "I like our new direction."

When night falls, we stop at a small patch of trees covered in green. The leaves hold yellows and oranges in their centers, and the patch of trees is surrounded by pines with tiny green needles. The sky rumbles as we explore our new horizons through the small forest. Kye occasionally reaches for the small of my back and points me to wildlife creeping about. And I let him.

Squirrels climb trees. Crickets sing to imaginary drumbeats, and birds, actual birds, talk to each other in the sky.

I laugh and head deeper into the thicket. He smiles as he moves past me, and I can't help but grab his hand as he passes. The small gesture, the small feel of laughter, crumbles in my heart. It glues my feet into the shrubbery beneath us and tears a new wound into my chest. "Kye?"

He stops and turns to me. "Yeah?"

"Do you think Josh is dead?"

His cheeks tighten at my question, and his body reacts in silence. I can't help but rush to him and fold myself into his arms. I crease my face into his neck, and there I stay as his breathing becomes heavier.

His body softens, and he pulls back, lifting my chin with his finger. Brushing his lips against mine, I feel a rush of butterflies through my body. Before I recover, he pulls back and wipes the tears from my eyes. "But I've been wrong before."

Finding a small pond about a mile west of the car, we sit and stare at the water, once more looking at ripples caused by the life living underneath. "We should move the Jeep to this spot. Clean and collect as much water as we can. Maybe even set up a camp and attempt to cook some fish," he says.

"What if it's not safe?"

"Then we make it safe. We boil it for as long as it takes. We burn the disease out of anything we cook. People did it once before; we can do it, too."

"People failed, Kye. People failed, and people died."

"The difference is patience. They were at war and had none. We have nothing holding us back."

The brush by the other side of the small pond rustles, and a small brown doe wanders out of its hiding place and grazes the water with her snout. She looks up at us for a moment, then drops her head and laps the blue water into her mouth.

"I will always take the first sip—anything ever placed before you. I will try it first. You'll know it's okay when you see me swallow it with no sour taste in my mouth. It will be a secret between you and me. No one ever has to know."

Chapter 31

Any water usage deemed unfit for the restoration of the

United Regions will be subject to review by local

enforcement offices.

We stay for three days. We drink the water, and we cook fish. Real fish. No packaged food or sandy appetizers. We build a fire to keep us warm at night, and Kye sings as the sun sets each night. On the third night, we fold into the back seat of the Jeep together, and I sleep to the soft beating of his heart. On day four, we collect as much water as we can and head farther South.

We are there within the hour.

The smell hits me first, the humid salt coming through my pores. At first, I think it's a dream, and I'm smelling the after-effects of all the fish we ate for days.

I hear it next, the small crash and beat of rushing water, the repeated soft thunder of the water on the ground.

And then I finally see it. The golden sand ripples like hills until it melts into each cascading wave's blue and white foam. The height of them stops me breathless. I watch as the water hits the rocky bay.

All we can do is walk toward it in disbelief. The safety of the Jeep suddenly feels stifling, and we enjoy the fresh air and the moisture from the ocean on our faces. I still can't move very fast, but Kye does not mind. We embrace every second.

Just east of the water is a small compound. Wooden houses encircle the entire beach, with people out and about, walking in all directions. Their feet are barefoot in the sand, their shoulders tanned from the sun.

Without fear, we go to them. We approach without the fear of laws we are breaking or the fear we won't be accepted.

One at a time, they stop to look at us. Some even smile and nod a silent welcome.

I remain in awe at the birds caressing the top of the water, the beautiful songs that ring from their beaks, and the unimaginable color of the salty sea that lay in front of me. Leaving our sorrows behind, we walk towards the gathering people crowding around us.

Kye and I grasp hands as the tears begin to flow down my face. His footsteps are timid, much like my own, but we don't stop. His grip on my hand is firm, much like the first night we spent together. I can't help but feel pride that he stands here with me. Even prouder as I see the admiration in his eyes for what lay in front of us.

We walk through the group and toward the water. We bend down to run the grainy sand through our fingertips. The people around us smile as an old and wrinkled woman bends down and begins to caress the sand in her fingertips.

"Please, take your time," she says. "When you're ready, make your way to the camp center, and we can make introductions. If you're willing to stay, we will make accommodations. From the looks of it, you must have had quite a long trip."

I drop to sit in the sand, overcome with thanks.

Kye drops to his knees, a sob of relief escaping his lungs. "I didn't actually think it was possible," he whispers.

My mind races. I see the sandy blond hair stumbling up the beach, his strides no larger than the length of his body. Maddox races up behind him, his knowing grin teasing me with his eyes, telling me he always knew. He knew I would find my way and find my way back to Austin. Find my way to the beach, just like Tommy always promised.

Austin jumps into my arms while my face sinks into the nape of his neck.

"Welcome home, Sara," he says. "Welcome home."

"The day you were born, the sky sang out with joy. The clouds danced directly towards the ocean across the breeze to announce your arrival." My mom brushes my hair as she gets me ready for bed, her voice as soft as the feathers on my pillow.

"Why the ocean, Ma? We don't live anywhere near the ocean."

"The ocean started as the purest place here on Earth. It's where the animals were born, where the mountains formed, and where all souls float, ready to start their new futures."

"Is it still that way?"

"No, my dear. Once the water wars ended, the oceans were cut off from the rest of the world. At first, the wind cried. But after some time, we learned new ways."

"I wish I could go to the ocean one day," I say.

"Me too, darling. Me, too."